Praise for *The Greek*

"A fast-paced slice of Romani ace".
— Sarah Ward, auth

"Bogdan Hrib writes with great vividness, and an inexorable grasp of narrative"
— Barry Forshaw, author, *Euro Noir*

"Bogdan Hrib's *The Greek Connection* is a remarkable staccato-paced journey through the Balkan mindset filled with an eclectic ensemble of unforgettable characters."
— Jeffrey Siger, International best selling author of the Chief Inspector Andreas Kaldis series.

"If this is the sharp taste of Balkan Noir, let's hope there's more to come."
— Quentin Bates, author of *Chilled to the Bone*.

Praise for Bogdan Hrib's Previous Novels:

"An exciting and suspenseful thriller. It is also a complex and detailed character study of an individual—a roller coaster ride through the transitions which have taken place over the last decades in Romanian history.
— Mike Phillips, author of *The Late Candidate*, winner of the Crime Writers' Association Silver Dagger Award

"... good reads offering an insight into a country that remains mysterious to many of us."
— Julian Cole, *The Press*, York

"... an exciting thriller. It is certain that Bogdan Hrib can write and that his translators have done a great job."
— Gisela Lehmer, *Crime Chronicles*

THE GREEK CONNECTION

Library and Archives Canada Cataloguing in Publication

Hrib, Bogdan
[Filiera greceasca. English]
    The Greek connection / written by Bogdan Hrib ; translated by Monica Ramirez.

Translation of: Filiera grecească.
Issued in print and electronic formats.
ISBN 978-1-77161-144-2 (pbk.).--ISBN 978-1-77161-145-9 (html).--ISBN 978-1-77161-146-6 (pdf)

    I. Title. II. Title: Filiera greceasca. English

PC840.418.R53F55 2015   859'.335   C2015-901690-8
                                                 C2015-901691-6

Pubished by Mosaic Press, Oakville, Ontario, Canada, 2015.
Distributed in the United States by Bookmasters (www.bookmasters.com).
Distributed in the U.K. by Gazelle Book Services (www.gazellebookservices.co.uk).

MOSAIC PRESS, Publishers
Copyright © 2015, Bogdan Hrib
Printed and Bound in Canada.
Design and layout by Eric Normann

Mosaic Press recognizes the support of the Ontario media Development Corporation, OMDC, for our publshing efforts.

We acknowledge the Ontario Arts Council
for their support of our publishing program

ONTARIO ARTS COUNCIL
CONSEIL DES ARTS DE L'ONTARIO
an Ontario government agency
un organisme du gouvernement de l'Ontario

We acknowledge the financial support of the Government of Canada through the Canada Book Fund (CBF) for this project.

Nous reconnaissons l'aide financière du gouvernement du Canada par l'entremise du Fonds du livre du Canada (FLC) pour ce projet.

 Canadian   Patrimoine
         Heritage   canadien

Canadä

MOSAIC PRESS
1252 Speers Road, Units 1 & 2
Oakville, Ontario L6L 5N9
phone: (905) 825-2130

info@mosaic-press.com

www.mosaic-press.com

THE GREEK CONNECTION

BOGDAN HRIB

translated
by Monica Ramirez

With the kind support of
the Romanian Cultural Institute

ROMANIAN
CULTURAL
INSTITUTE

Also by Bogdan Hrib

Stelian Munteanu series:

Filiera grecească (Book 1, 2007, Tritonic Publishing Group, 2009, Crime Scene Publishing);

Blestemul manuscrisului (co-author with Răzvan Dolea, Book 2, 2008, 2010, Tritonic Publishing Group);

Somalia, Mon Amour (Book 3, 2009, Tritonic Publishing Group);

Ucideți generalul (Book 4, 2011, Tritonic Publishing Group);

Kill the General (2011, ProFusion Crime, London, UK);

3+1, stories (2013, Tritonic Publishing Group).

Stand alones:

Ultima fotografie (2012, Cartea Românească)

Terapie pentru crimă (co-author with Kiki Vasilescu – 2014, Tritonic Publishing Group).

To my little family

List of characters

Stelian Munteanu, Romanian, age forty, freelance journalist, book editor, working as a spokesman for the Romanian Police, an occasional adventurer, 1.78 meters tall, chestnut brown hair streaked with grey green eyes, short hair. He sometimes wears a moustache. A sniper during his army service.

Galia Kalughina, Russian, early twenties, she is a dancer in a prominent Bucharest nightclub, friend of the victim.

Tatiana (Tania) Sevcenko, Russian, age about twenty-five, dancer, victim.

Mircea Popescu, Romanian, late fifties, businessman after the Romanian Revolution, very wealthy and very well-connected.

Nora Popescu, Romanian, his wife, fifteen years younger than her husband, formerly a lawyer but now a wealthy housewife.

Dan Manole, Romanian, age about twenty-five, brother of Nora Popescu, major suspect.

Iannis Theodopoulos, Greek, Police Chief Inspector in Paralia, Katerini. He needs some glasses for reading and he is very tired. Likes to eat seafood. He does not like the summer season, too many tourists.

Eleni Papastergiu, Greek, age thirty, single, Professor at Thessaloniki University and specialist in mineralogy - She knows everything there is to know about stones and jewels.

Mikhail (Misha) Sergeyevich Pushkin, Russian, early sixties, former FSB, KGB and maybe MI6, knows everything and appears whenever he's not expected. A key character who puts in occassional appearances. Smokes cigarettes. Good with a gun and behind the wheel of a car.

Jacques Sardi, French, early forties, *Inspecteur de Police a Paris*, a department dealing with acquisitive crime. He does not love Russians but he loves beautiful women and expensive cars.

Anton (Toni) Demetriade, Romanian, early thirties, police inspector in Bucharest, investigation partner of Stelian's. Drives an old-fashioned Romanian Dacia 1310.

Steiner, Austrian, age fifty, chief inspector in the Vienna police. Tall, white hair, doesn't say much.

ONE

STELIAN MUNTEANU HAS A BAD FEELING THAT HE CAN'T QUITE kick, let alone put into words. He shouldn't complain. It's the third day of his vacation, and he's finally out of Bucharest. He's gone to the sea, in Greece, and thankfully far away from his co-workers, boss and neighbours, not to mention Bucharest's crazy drivers. *So what's the problem then? Loneliness? ohhhh …*

The sun has set, but the sky is still painted in pastel hues of blue and red. The air is hot and still. Faint white clouds wander over the horizon like a scene pulled from an old watercolour. Only a high flying jet cutting a straight pink line breaks the otherwise splendid scene. *Peace and serenity.*

The room has air conditioning, but he hasn't switched it on. He might have to tonight, if this heat doesn't die down. After a long relaxing shower, he steps out onto the balcony with a fluffy white towel draped around his waist. The main street two floors below has only just come alive. Billboards and shop signs slowly light up one by one. Up above, the resort town feels welcoming and refined. The place is clean; no screaming, no rowdy drunks. A symphony of languages echoes from the hotels and tavernas. There seems to be a lot of Romanian these days.

Yet this depression is overwhelming.

"Too many years without a decent vacation. Then there's the stress, the exhaustion, the divorce…"

1

As he leans against the railing of Paralia's Elektra Beach Hotel, he feels a little ridiculous complaining to the wind on such a beautiful September evening. Just as he starts scolding himself everything suddenly fades to black. The power is out.

Shit, just what I need! It's not enough that I'm here dateless, now I'm going to starve to death. Some vacation.

He steps back into the room to look for a flashlight or matches. *What's the point? It's not like I'm going to light candles…celebrate loneliness and a forced fasting.* He remembers the flashlight in his suitcase. You never know when you might need one…the flashlight, a penknife, some string. *A silly habit from when I was young…*

Suddenly, he looks into the darkness outside to a building across the street. There's a hotel painted in traditional white and blue, that was probably chic at one time but is now locked up and empty for some reason. He can see streaks of light darting from window to window on the first floor. He tries to get a better look.

Always on the job!

It takes him a while to find the flashlight in his suitcase, and by the time he does the lights start flickering and the power comes back to life. Adjusting his eyes, the powerful street lights outside blind him, and the chaos strips away the previous calm.

He looks at his watch and decides it's time to go out. He gets dressed in a pair of beige pants and a brown shirt. Brown shoes as well. He leaves his papers in the suitcase, removes a fifty from his wallet and sticks his room key in his pocket. He takes a last critical look at himself in the mirror.

Just before leaving his room he remembers the strange lights in the windows. He can't see anything suspicious anymore. *Let the games begin. Maybe I'll be lucky tonight.*

Galia Kalughina is too bored to wait for her roommate anymore. It's late and the tourists are already out for the evening stroll. And she's still mad about the blackout—she was stuck in the darkness of the shower with shampoo in her hair. She hit her head on the shower head, soap fell in the bathtub and she slipped. When she got out to look for a lighter, she tripped across the floor, only stopping when her nose hit a mirror. There were plenty of obstacles invisible in the darkness: an armchair, a suitcase ... What a catastrophe!

When the lights turned back on, she was close to tears.

The room is a disaster. On both beds, hers and Tania's, there are huge piles of brightly coloured clothes: tank-tops, skirts, trousers, sexy lingerie and shawls. A make-up case spilled all over the small desk. Body creams, shampoos, bottles with nail paint and perfumes. It's enough for an army of cheerleaders let alone two girls. But they're on vacation and here to have fun.

That's it, I've waited long enough. I'll leave her the key at the reception and she'll have to manage from there. At least she could have told me where she was going so I could make my own plans.

She's had her eyes on a Polish guy, or maybe he was a Czech, she wasn't too sure, who was a regular at the Poseidon, a Greek *taverna* that specialized in seafood.

She's certain that Tania has met up with that dreamy Romanian guy again, that one she has kept a secret. *Her business, her life!* She sighs and slips on a burgundy skirt and a pink tank-top showing a generous amount of cleavage, over a Triumph bra, for which she paid almost as the cost of the whole vacation. But it's worth every penny; the effect is devastating. For the finishing touches, she puts on a silver Greek necklace, matching earrings and a thick ring with a beautiful amethyst stone. High heels with white straps. A last touch-up of her make-up, a little hair spray and a touch of *Lancôme Magie Noir*, and she's ready. To the dance floor!

Galia wants to enjoy her vacation to its fullest. She knows she's irresistible.

She descends the stairs from the third floor and heads towards the Poseidon. She bumps into a man dressed in dreary colours with a lost look on his face. Galia mumbles something in Russian and the man apologizes in an unknown language. He's out of her head in seconds, as she's already turned her thoughts to the Polish guy—or Czech or... whatever—he's her target tonight.

Iannis Theodopoulos has just finished a long report and feels like his eyes will jump out of their sockets. There's no paperwork in the movies. *Cops don't do anything except arrest bad guys armed with machine-guns and seduce beautiful blondes accused of murder.*

He stands, his body almost numb, and looks out the window of his first floor office. Hordes of tourists are taking in the city. They look happy, maybe a bit too happy, except for a forty-something guy dressed in brown clothes, who looks totally out of place as he walks aimlessly. He's surrounded by balloons, souvlaki-to-go, tiny tank-tops and sun hats…

Looks like he's too tired, or too drunk… Or both… He erases the weird guy from his head.

Theodopoulos's office is just an ordinary provincial police station, the only one in Paralia. The furniture is plastic and far from new. There are faded white computers with old monitors covered in yellow and green post-it notes. The place fits all the cop stereotypes—files everywhere, scattered stationary, a dog-eared diary left open to yesterday's date and several mugs caked in remnants of old coffee. A massive desk lamp with a blue lampshade is adorned with an enormous chain filled with keys hanging in plain view. Everything looks normal, but somehow foggy.

I should go and get my eyes checked. It's a sign I'm getting old.

The busy day is over and he's the only one left in the office. It's the night shift. He knows he won't get a vacation, not until the fall; the whole coast is packed with tourists and something terrible could happen at any moment. *God forbid…*

Iannis Theodopoulos stuffs his files inside a bag he collects from the floor, thinking ahead to the hot meal waiting for him at home. *There's another sign I'm getting old…Here's me thinking about food instead of thinking about my wife.*

With a bored sigh he stands, just as the phone starts to ring. He looks at it perplexed and pretends he doesn't hear it. *Is it a dream? A nightmare? What the hell do they want at this time of night?* But it keeps ringing, and somehow it sounds like it's getting louder. He sighs again, sits back down and drops the bag on the floor, then snatches the receiver.

"Hello?"

Mircea Popescu has just finished his first glass of Metaxa Seven Stars. The caramel coloured liquid fills washes over his tongue and senses with its velvety aroma. He's trying to lose weight by replacing his two daily beers with two daily glasses of cognac. It's an expensive choice, but Mircea Popescu can afford it.

The terrace he's on belongs to an expensive restaurant, a very expensive restaurant with stylish waiters dressed to impress. The white tablecloths aren't made of cheap paper. There's rattan furniture, soft lights and lots of candles. Precious patrons. Expensive suits and ties. Golden watches, bracelets sprinkled with diamonds. Lots of money. Snobs. Idle chit-chat in low tones. Discreet background music of the café-concert type, not Greek.

"Don't you think it's a bit much every night?!"

His wife, Nora Popescu, tactfully tries to maintain the internal balance of this impassive man. Now, most of her diplomacy has been abandoned. She's waiting for her brother and he's late for dinner. And it's not for the first time. She also knows that Mircea is hungry and going to erupt soon. She's almost fifteen years younger than he is and sometimes the difference shows.

"Leave me alone!"

She'd decided to accept his marriage proposal more for financial reasons than because of any real affection. Ten years had passed since then and she's wondering more and more if she didn't make a big mistake. *Still, I used to love him... What happened? His business? All those months when he's away? The mystery man that the press spun? Politics? Other women?* When she gets to this question she prefers to stop her train of thought. She sighs.

"Dan never told you what time he was coming did he, Mircea?"

"Since when does Dan tell me anything?! If he doesn't show up in half an hour, I'll go look for him."

It's not such a great night for the Popescu family. Nora glances around, trying not to lose her patience. At the entrance, a lonely guy of middle age studies the prices on the menu. He's dressed in plain brownie clothes. His eyes are glassy... *Poor and lost in space.*

The guy turns around and leaves. Nora is still looking for a handsome and happy man. *Someone more upbeat and not as repugnant as all the men I meet. Where have all the courteous and good humoured men disappeared to?*

Misha Pushkin is smoking on the street while he walks. He's trying to keep his cigarette as close to his body as he can so as not accidentally burn someone. He's an ordinary guy, nothing about him attracts any kind of attention. His hair is almost completely white, his face not too wrinkled and he's freshly shaved. His deep blue eyes are sharp and alive. He wears white pants and a shirt striped in two shades of blue, and blue sport shoes. He looks like a retired naval officer.

A man crosses his path, almost bumping into him, staring straight ahead. Misha steps aside and looks over his shoulder, keeping the man in his line of sight. He memorizes his face and silhouette. *Almost looked like a potential victim. You never know…*

He's just arrived and intuition tells him that things will start to happen soon. *Someone has to make the first move. All the players are already set. Who will act first? How and when?* He misses the fight. His muscles are tense, as if waiting for something. But in the meantime, the evening stroll does him a lot of good, just like a fine cigarette, or coffee.

Misha Pushkin doesn't talk much, he doesn't act much, but he always shows up at the right time. Just like the old saying: right place, right time!

I should plan for a little trip to Salonica tomorrow. To visit the White Tower and look for an old contact.

Eleni Papastergiu feels tired. The movie she has just finished watching on TV was nothing special, some Hugh Grant and Julia Roberts romantic comedy set in leafy bohemian London. He's a librarian, she's a famous actress, and of course there's the mandatory happy-ending. The air is cool in her little apartment and it's dark. She's had a difficult day at the University, teaching courses for preparatory classes before attending a teachers' briefing in the evening. All very tedious on a hot mid-summer's day. Financially speaking, summer school was a good idea, but it certainly didn't make her happy.

We don't even get any extra money for it.

She can see a corner of the illuminated harbour and part of the White Tower from her living room window. It's past midnight and the night life is in full swing. She considers going out to Maxi's to catch up with some friends over drinks, but sleep sounds like a better option right now.

Eleni's days flow with an almost precise routine. Alone in a big university city, she's surrounded by her books and stones.

Another movie starts on the TV. Instead of London, this cheesy romance is set in Paris and sprinkled with images of the Eiffel Tower and the Place de la Concorde. She turns off the TV and tries to sleep. *Ohhh, too many stereotypes... Love stories and famous European capitals. Where do I find a man like that? Paris, London? Are there no more available men in Salonica?*

Jacques Sardi is savouring his wine. Red, evidently. And dry. French.

From the last floor of the Arch on La Defense, he can see all the way to the Arch de Triumph on Place Charles de Gaulle. With a stretch of his imagination, he can even glimpse the Obelisque from Place de la Concorde. The view is gorgeous and he delights in it every time he sees it, thankful that he had been born in this wonderful city. It's like a gift from God to make up for his unhappy childhood. *I nearly forgot those years...*

The little soirée is winding down. The guests are a mixed crowd, but he's managed to find a few interesting people to speak to, all of them women. They're respectable ladies wearing enormous necklaces adorned with diamonds and sapphires. All young and shy, but throwing inviting glances his way while shaking their long, white-gold and diamond earrings. Everywhere he looks he can see wealth and expensive jewelry.

He sighs and glances at his image in the mirror. Not too bad at all. Black suit, white shirt with the last button left undone, straight posture, no belly, fair skin. Black hair and green eyes. Maybe he should start to consider a serious relationship. *Well... isn't it too early? There's still time...*

He tries to figure out a way home; should he cut through the center all the way to the Rue Ranelagh, or take a road around the city's outskirts? Paris is filled with tourists, and it's hot this time of year. Like usual, he has a lot of work to do. It's a long time since he's been to his little countryside villa; maybe next weekend.

He approaches the elevator that will take him to the parking lot, where he parked his old black Peugeot 307. Too bad he's not on duty. He could switch on the siren and flashing lights and would it would get him home a lot faster. Before stepping into the elevator, he places his glass on an empty tray and switches his cell phone from mute to normal.

Maybe someone will call, it's still too early to go to bed...

TWO

A LOUD BUZZING NOISE, STRANGELY METALLIC, FILLS THE room. He hides his throbbing head under the pillow. He probably had too much Imiglikos and cheap cognac last night. *It's the best way to drink when you're on such low pay.*

The sunlight blinds him despite the heavy curtains. He closes his eyes.

"What the hell! Who's calling at this hour?"

He knows it's not an alarm clock, since he forgot his back in Bucharest. *A phone call? The reception? Don't they have anything else to do?*

He glances dumbfounded at the nightstand and sees that it's his cell phone. He grabs it and narrows his eyes. He reads the number on the screen, but doesn't recognize it. He wonders if he should answer it. *What if it's something urgent?*

"Hello?"

"Did I wake you?"

Everything falls apart like a house of cards. *Stupid cliché. Like when I used to work for the newspaper.* He recognizes the voice knowing that this is not going to be good.

"Yes. Honestly, yes…"

"I'm sorry. I'm not calling to chat."

"I can imagine. What number are you calling me from? I don't recognize it."

"Well, some numbers have changed. Doesn't matter. We have a problem."

"I can only be happy about it, boss. I've just started my vacation."

"We're not calling you back. There's a problem in Paralia."

"Here?"

"Yes, a murder."

"A murder in Paralia?! You have to be kidding."

"Pay attention and try to concentrate!"

"Okay, okay, I'm listening."

"There's a Romanian citizen involved. They've asked for a representative of Romania to assist them with the investigation. It might just be a mistake. I didn't really get everything they were saying. You'll have to check it out."

"But I'm not a detective, boss!"

"Look, a journalist is better than nothing. You're expected at the police station in Paralia. Do you know where that is?"

"I think so. I've seen a police station close to my hotel, right at the end of the street."

"Good. It's ten past seven. Detective Theodopoulos is expecting you there at eight. I'll call you later for news."

The connection dies.

"Murder in Paralia?!" It seemed incredible.

He throws the phone down on the bed and tries to stand up on his wobbly legs. *Some vacation. This is the last thing I needed. Work, work, work. Just like the old days…* He takes a step toward the bathroom, but trips on his slippers and then his suitcase. He rummages for his toiletries and makes his way toward the bathroom. It's been two days without shaving and his stubble is really showing.

"What can a journalist masquerading as a detective do?!"
He starts to laugh and cuts himself with his razor.

Iannis pours another cup of coffee, his head feeling like a church bell. *How many cups of coffee?* He looks at his watch, noticing that there are only a few minutes left until eight. *I wonder if he'll show up on time.* He hadn't slept all night, trying to make some sense of this very weird business. He had only dozed off in his chair for a few minutes, but his eyes felt heavy with sleep. *Glasses, I need glasses! I can't delay anymore!*

"Good morning, sir. My name is Munteanu, from the Romanian Police.

Iannis jumps and almost spills his coffee.

"Good morning," he growls. "I was waiting for you. Iannis Theodopoulos. Take a seat."

"Thank you."

Except for the sounds of the waves on the beach, the office is like most police stations, well lit and austere.

"I'm listening, mister Theodopoulos."

Iannis studies Munteanu. He looked just as dizzy as Iannis felt. Like the situation had taken him by surprise. Without intending to, he takes a liking to the man.

"Please, call me Iannis. It's easier. We're colleagues, after all."

Munteanu approves with a crooked smile.

"Indeed. Stelian, or Stelios for you. So, what's with all this drama?"

"The drama is a murder!"

"I'm listening."

"It's a short story, really. Someone saw lights on inside the Alkion Hotel and tried to contact the owner. The place has been closed for a while and is the subject of litigation, so everyone keeps a close eye on it. It's right across the street from us."

"Yes, I've seen it. I am staying just down the street at the Elektra Beach Hotel."

"Anyway, someone came by representing the owners and called the police. They suspected thieves. Obviously, we weren't far away.

We found the door to the beach entrance was open and found the victim inside. A woman. She was holding a note with only two words: *Themis five*. Your countryman, Daniel Manole, is checked in at the Themis Hotel, room five."

"When did all of this happen?"

"A little after midnight."

"And do we know where Manole was at that time?"

"In his room. Apparently changing, or packing. Very nervous."

"And now?"

"He's here. We've kept him isolated in a room all night. We don't have a jail in here."

"Who's the victim?"

"Russian girl. Tatiana Sevcenko."

"And what reason would he have for killing her?"

"I don't think it's that simple. Manole refused to give any kind of statement until we bring someone representing the Romanian authorities. It seems that you were the closest."

"Yes, really close. I saw a light inside the Alkion Hotel too. Maybe a flashlight, maybe even two."

"What time?"

"During the blackout."

"Interesting. Was the light moving?"

"It gave me the feeling like someone was searching for something. It moved from right to left. Why did you request a Romanian detective for this investigation?"

"We didn't. But it seems that Mister Manole has very powerful relatives. Someone interfered in the Foreign Ministry and requested a representative of Romanian authority."

"Interesting. What a mess."

"Don't even go there. I've been awake the whole night, reporting right and left."

"I'm innocent. I was on vacation."

The Greek sips from his now cold coffee. A moment of silence, then he starts again, "Well, I think you should talk to Manole. But just so you know, the conversation will be recorded."

"That's fine. Thanks for warning me."

"We're colleagues…"

"Is he here with anyone else?"

"Yes. His sister and brother-in-law, Nora and Mircea Popescu. This Popescu guy seems to be extremely influential in Romania. He's the one who demanded a Romanian."

"There are many Popescus in Romania, but his name doesn't ring a bell with me."

"Okay. Follow me."

The room where Manole is being held is a cross between a dull jail cell and an old college dorm room like the ones Stelian remembered from the Grozavesti district back in Bucharest.

Actually, I haven't been at that campus much, so my memory might be playing tricks on me, thought Stelian.

Colourless inlay floors, a metal-barred window and a metal-framed bed, all of the room's grey walls are adorned with bright posters of palm trees and shiny beaches, hotels and yachts with the ever-present slogan: *Discover the Greek Islands!*

With a smile and a cold shiver, Stelian enters and gets his first look at Daniel Manole, who's seated at a table in the centre of the room. He suddenly realizes that he'd just been staring at Thedopoulos's coffee without asking for a one. Not that one was offered. *It's going to be a difficult morning without a large, strong coffee. Ohhh…this life is so unfair… You're complaining again, Stelică! Worse, you're whining!* He shakes his head to clear his thoughts.

"Good morning, Mister Manole."

"Finally. You're Romanian, right?"

"Yes. I'm Romanian."

"I'm glad. I'd rather have a Romanian policeman."

"Well, I don't want to disappoint you, but I'm only the spokesman of the police."

"Spokesman? Shouldn't they send an agent or something?"

Stelian sighs, exasperated. He scratches his head and blinks nervously, repeating the same thing he had said earlier to the Greek detective, "I was the closest person available."

"Closest to what? I don't understand!"

"It's rather simple. There was no way to find a Romanian policeman right here in Paralia on such short notice. I was here on vacation, checked in at a hotel less than a hundred meters from the police station..."

"Whatever. So how can you help me? I'm innocent!"

Stelian takes a seat on the opposite chair. He rubs his face with his hands, hoping to chase away the cobwebs caused by interrupted sleep. Outside, the heat is unbearable. He looks around, searching for air conditioning. Nothing. He sighs again. Daniel Manole is a young man. He's too young. He lacks patience and is an idealist with an influential brother-in-law. *This is going to be one hell of a long investigation, so I can kiss my vacation goodbye. That's me, the luckiest man alive...* He takes out a pen, notebook and a digital recorder from his pocket and places them on the table.

"I'm sorry. I'm really a journalist, so I can't help it. My name is Stelian Munteanu. I'm listening."

He starts the recorder and gestures for Manole to go on.

"Where should I start?"

"Let's do it the standard way. First give your name and age."

"Daniel Ioan Manole, twenty-three years old."

"Great. Go on, please."

"We're being recorded, right? I mean, by them as well?"

"Of course. How did you meet the victim, Tatiana?"

"Tatiana? We were friends. I mean more than friends."

"Where did you meet her?"

"Here."

"And that would be..."

"In a bar."

Stelian is growing angry. Manole is wasting his time. It's hot and he should be on the beach.

"Mister Manole, I'm trying to help you. Your situation doesn't look good. You're the primary suspect in a murder case. So please cooperate and don't force me to drag every word out of your mouth!"

With that, the young man looks him in the eye for the first time. Fear starts to blossom in his eyes.

"Look, I don't want to be tough on you. But the sooner we set things straight, the sooner you can return to your family. After all, you're on vacation. Just like me."

"So you believe that I'm innocent?"

"For now, I don't believe anything. I'm only listening."

"Okay, I'm trying. I met Tania a week ago. It was love at first sight for the both of us. She spoke Romanian, and was a dancer in a nightclub back in Bucharest. We spent a lot of time together. We made plans. We were going to get married."

"Love at first sight? Marriage? After only a week?"

"You've never been in love? We wanted to run away together. Tania has relatives in Paris. We were going to settle down there, get jobs."

Stelian drifts off into deep thought. *In love?! Have I ever been in love? Or at least have I ever thought I was in love? What does love really mean?*

Daniel's eyes fill with tears.

"Look, I'm afraid and I didn't even do anything. We were hiding in that abandoned hotel. We didn't do anything wrong, didn't bother anyone. We found an way in and bought a small bottle of Metaxa and two ice-creams. We had candles. It was romantic. But we ran out of cigarettes. I went out to buy some... I was only gone for a few minutes. When I came back I found her on the floor. She wasn't moving. Something had happened. I called her name, I tried to wake her up and then I felt her pulse. I couldn't feel anything. I got scared and I ran. I don't know anything after that. That's the truth, I give you my word."

Stelian sighs for maybe the thousandth time. He bites the pen, stops the recorder and growls. *The hell with it! I'm in deep shit!*

"Okay, stay here. I'll be right back."

Only after the words have left his lips does he understand their stupidity, but Manole is already absently staring out the window and doesn't seem to have heard. Outside, the cries of the seagulls and the noise of children playing on the beach blend into a universal song; and now it's even hotter.

Iannis places a cup of hot coffee and a glass of iced water in front of him. Three huge ice cubes slowly melt in the glass. *This combination is murderous! A cold beer would be better!*

"So, did you clarify things?"

Stelian shakes his head. *Clarify things my ass!*

"I don't understand what happened."

"Is he innocent?" asks the Greek. "What do you think?"

"I'm inclined to believe him. He didn't have an obvious reason to kill her. Do we know how she was killed?"

"No sign of violence. Apparently it was poison. We'll know more soon enough."

"Today?"

"Yes. Do you want to see the body?"

"Honestly, not really. Is it necessary?"

"No, it's not. The fact of the matter is that there are no visible marks. She's with the forensic guys right now, they do all kinds of tests. A beautiful girl. Poisoned. The Metaxa seems to have contained a very powerful poison. Possibly cyanide. It's the most common."

"Honestly, I haven't heard of a murder by poisoning lately. Too intellectual. Seems like it was taken out of an Agatha Christie novel."

"She drank it without suspecting anything. Death was probably instantaneous. A quiet and efficient method."

"Are there any other suspects?"

"Tania had a girlfriend, Galia. They stayed in the same hotel room. But it seems she wasn't in the room last night. Maybe she was out, partying in the clubs. We left word at the reception that we're waiting to speak to her when she gets back."

"What if she forgets to come? Or runs away?"

"She doesn't stand a chance. We'll get her."

"What did you find at the crime scene?"

"Here's the list."

"Could we go there?"

"Sure. We took all the fingerprints, but didn't move anything."

Sure thing, I'm not at my best today! Iannis stands and quickly swallows some water. Very cold. He leaves the coffee untouched.

Nora Popescu smokes cigarette after cigarette. She only smokes half of each, and then crushes it into the ashtray before lighting another.

"Didn't you quit? What has gotten into you? Anyways, smoking is forbidden inside the hotel!"

She ignores her husband and lights another. Her hands are shaking. The flame of the lighter vibrates. Smoke and tension fill the air.

"Mircea, when is Bucharest calling you?"

Her husband is sweaty, unshaved, with a towel around his neck and a Blackberry in his left hand.

"Don't stress me out, please! They promised they'll take care of everything. It seems that one of our cops is right here in Paralia."

"What's his name?"

"I don't know. We'll find out soon. Just put out your cigarette, you'll burn this place down. Calm down."

"How can I calm down? Dan has been arrested!"

"No hysterics. We'll take care of it. Look, I'm going to take a shower. Stay next to the phone and check your email."

He disappears into the bathroom and turns on the water. Nora crushes another cigarette into the ashtray. She searches the package for another one. It's empty. She feels like crying. She's furious. Arrested! Murder! How is that possible? What kind of country is this?! My brother, the kindest man alive! She crushes the empty cigarette package in her fist and throws it on the floor.

* * *

The abandoned hotel has a mysterious feel to it. Opened doors with chipped paint, dark, deserted hallways, empty rooms with dirty walls showing marks of long gone furniture. Dust and musty air.

It's almost like we're waiting for some ghosts to appear any moment now. Brr... I wonder what stops the owners from opening again. Now it's going to be even harder to draw guests with a murder on record. Or not. Who knows, maybe they can use it as a smart marketing campaign. It could become a touristic attraction. I could write a book... Murder in Paralia. Yeah, and who would care?

Their steps echo through the marble hallway of the ground-floor. Spread on the floor are a few objects surrounding the victim's outline, drawn by the Greek police. An icy shiver runs through Stelian as he leans against the railing. With every minute that passes he becomes more aware that this is more than a bad dream, but something real, and things are not as simple as he'd been inclined to think. And it was too difficult to explain to Iannis that he's actually a journalist, and forensic investigations are not really his cup of tea. *Too late now... I've started the game and I have to play it to the end.*

"Everything is in place," says Iannis.

A nearly empty bottle of cognac and two glasses, a dusty fur coat, two empty plastic containers with plastic spoons, a black flashlight, a crushed cigarette pack, a full ashtray, a small notebook with a long pencil, a CD player and a lighter.

"Nothing's missing?"

He quickly regrets the foolish question. But in all honesty, he is at a loss about what else he should ask.

"Only the piece of paper found in the victim's hand with the two words: *Themis five.* It was torn from that notebook," replies the detective.

"That's very weird. What would she need that information for? She knew where Manole was staying. Maybe she wanted to give it to someone, but it's hard to believe that two young lovers would think about anyone else while in each other's arms. And what were they doing with a notebook and pencil? Were they planning to write something? They had each other..."

"Well, I don't know if the feeling of love was mutual. Looks like the victim had a lot of money, and that's suspicious, especially at her age. I think there's a husband, or rich lover in the picture. Some kind of a protector."

"Are you trying to tell me that Manole fell in love with a high class prostitute?"

"No, I'm only saying that she apparently had a lot of money. This fur coat must be worth around two thousand euros."

Stelian smiles. In Paralia, all the locals are fur coat specialists. Two days ago he had visited shops where all the sales people wanted to give him details about the luxurious goods on their shelves. *Who the hell buys fur coats in this heat? Something like buying a sled in the summer and a bike in the winter…*

"Kind of expensive to be used as a carpet."

"They must have seen too many movies. All that was missing was a fireplace and some wood."

The conversation strays and Stelian realizes that he's becoming more cynical by the minute. *I didn't use to be this way. This is about someone's life!* He crouches and studies the floor. He remembers the investigation techniques used in the movies. *Maybe it'll even be interesting.*

"The marble is very dusty. There are many sets of foot prints. Anyone dealt with that yet?"

"We took pictures. Two sets of foot prints have already been identified: the victim's and Daniel's. But there's at least one more set, possibly belonging to the people who had called the police. We're not sure yet."

"What if it belongs to the actual murderer?"

"There are no signs of violence. The third party should have been someone they both knew. Besides, robbery is out of the question. Tania was wearing jewelry and the fur coat is worth a lot of money."

"Manole said he went out to buy cigarettes and when he came back he found her dead. He was only gone for a few minutes. If that's the case, then the theory that someone must have been watching them from inside of the hotel seems to be the most logical to me."

"Believe me, Stelios, I really don't want to have to accuse your countryman, but for now we don't have any other leads. There's no one else. Maybe only Tania's roommate."

"Still, don't you find the note in Tania's hand to be a little weird? She knew where Daniel's room was. It looks to me like it was placed there on purpose to send us off on the wrong path."

"Until we find a motive, we can't really think about who did it. At first I suspected jealousy."

"But who was jealous, Iannis? Don't you agree that there has to be a third party?"

The loud ringing of Iannis's cell phone interrupts the debate. Stelian doesn't know a word of Greek, so he has no idea what the short discussion is about.

"Let's go back to my office. Tania's roommate has shown up and is waiting for us."

"Wait a second. Shouldn't we take all these things so your people can look for fingerprints and any other clues? DNA? Sperm stains, maybe? I'm just saying…"

The Greek detective gives a bitter laugh as he wipes his sweaty forehead.

"You've been watching too many CSI episodes. We'll verify everything. I only wanted you to see the crime scene first. And don't forget that we're not in New York, and we're not starring in a cop show."

"Well, sue me for insisting, but did anyone check the fur coat?"

Theodopoulos shrugs.

"What for? It's obviously new. We found nothing in the pockets. Of course we looked at it, but there's nothing special about it. It's was bought here in Paralia. I saw the tag. We'll send it to the laboratory in Katerini. But as far as I know, we don't have the necessary equipment, so they'll get send it to Salonica. That'll take time and we can't afford to waste a minute. So let's go."

Still, why would you leave something new and so expensive on the floor? A romantic gesture? A glass of cognac on an expensive fur with your new lover? A fur with a two thousand euro price tag? Something's missing from this picture. Something's definitely not right…

THREE

wow…

The young woman sitting in the police station is stunning. A burgundy mini-skirt and a low-cut pink tank-top, assorted jewelry, high-heels, a daring look. Only her make-up is ruined. She's been crying. A Greek cop is taking care of the necessary translation and they are a few minutes into the discussion already. The table and two chairs are occupied. Stelian and Iannis take a seat on two additional chairs next to a wall covered with an enormous map of the Salonica coastline. On the side there's a water cooler and a huge metal locker. A second massive table is overflowing with files. A tall coat rack stands in the corner.

This doesn't look like a real interrogation room, more like a borrowed office. Maybe the archive room...

"Galia Kalughina, twenty-one years old, from Kiev," the young woman responds to the cop's questions.

"How long have you known the victim?"

"About a year, I think. We dance at the same nightclub in Bucharest."

"Do you know the man she was dating?"

"I've seen him a few times. Tania kept him all to herself, like a secret. She was afraid I would steal him from her. A Romanian... Daniel, something."

"Could you recognize him?"

"Of course."

"Did the victim have any other connections here in Paralia?"

"Here? No...I don't know."

"She never spoke to anyone else except for you and Daniel Manole?"

"I can't be sure. We weren't together all the time. But I think I saw her waving at two, or three other people."

"Men?"

"I wasn't really paying attention. I didn't care."

"Try to remember. Anyone in particular?"

"I've seen her talking once or twice with a tall, fat man, but he was wearing a hat and I couldn't see his face. Like I said, I didn't really pay attention."

Munteanu chuckled. *There's the third party. Simple, really! The hell she didn't notice. I bet she wanted to know all the details, but Tania wasn't telling her anything.*

"Did you notice anything that would indicate a close relationship between the victim and the stranger?"

"I don't know. I think I've seen them talking together twice. I couldn't hear anything, but I think they were arguing."

"Did you notice any violent gestures?"

"No."

"Could he be a relative of hers?"

"I don't think so. All her relatives are from St. Petersburg, why would they be here? Besides, she left Russia two years ago."

"Are you aware of any other relationships she might have had?"

"I don't understand."

"Any other friends or lovers who might have been here?"

"I'm not familiar with Tania's private life."

"Is there anything else of interest that you can tell us about the victim?"

"Nothing."

Munteanu turns towards Theodopoulos and whispers: "Can I step in?"

"Of course."

He passes his hand through his hair, trying to concentrate.

"Please ask her if Tania introduced her to any men in Bucharest."

The cop translated his question and her answer:

"I don't know any of Tania's friends, except for our colleagues at the nightclub. I didn't interfere in her life. Is that all? I would like to change," the young woman said, irritated.

"Please ask her if she remembers how the victim was given the fur coat."

The cop repeats the question.

"Given? She wasn't given it, she bought it herself. She's been saving money for almost a year for that."

"Thank you."

"Anything else? I need to change, I've been dancing all night."

"Please don't leave the city until the investigation is over. Good-bye."

The office is quiet now. They're alone. Theodopoulos looks at his watch.

"Do you really trust her not to leave the city? I'm kind of worried. I don't think she was completely honest with us."

Iannis looks at Munteanu with a tired but sly smile.

"We'll be watching her. I don't trust her at all. I'll get a sur-veillance team on her. So, what now? It's almost noon and I haven't eaten anything since this morning. Do you feel like an early lunch?"

Munteanu returned Iannis's smile. He had forgotten about his stomach, but now with the sudden reminder…

The Poseidon Taverna is a standard Greek restaurant, nothing high-class, but very clean and pleasant. A terrace with about ten tables and an open kitchen where a young cook juggles fish and other unknown marine creatures. A true seafood paradise. A waiter brings two menus, one in Greek for Iannis and one in English for Stelian. He opens it with a lost expression.

"I hope this place is okay with you," says Iannis.

Munteanu's head feels like he a freight train has driven through it. At a nearby table an overweight, Romanian family—father, mother and two sons—order pork steaks, French fries and beer, with hamburgers and cokes for the kids. The waiter stares at them irritated, since they probably don't have pork at a place called the Poseidon, but he doesn't comment. It's a funny feeling, but Munteanu feels embarrassed by his countrymen.

It's their problem, I won't start to educate them right now. How stupid to order pork when you can have fresh seafood. It's health-ier and…

"Hey, did you hear me? Are you okay? I brought you here because I thought you would like something special, like seafood. Octopus, oysters, mussels, you name it."

Stelian gives up on his inner thoughts.

"Yeah, I know. It's just kind of hard to enjoy this right now. I was at the beginning of my vacation and now it's all ruined."

"Were you alone?"

Stelian blushes, trying to look at the sea.

"Damn, I'm sorry," says Iannis. "I shouldn't have asked."

"No, don't worry about it. Yes, I'm alone. Divorced."

"I'm sorry."

"Well, it's for the best. The capitalist lifestyle pulled us away from each other. We didn't spend enough time together, always too busy with work in two completely different fields. I was poorer, she was fairly rich. Well, she had rich aunts. We separated amicably, but it's not easy to get used to being alone again. Even if we weren't spending too much time together, I still enjoyed the feeling that I wasn't alone. Now it's like I've lost a good part of my balance."

"Any kids?"

"Yes, a five-year-old little girl. Iulia. She lives with her mother…"

Stelian sighs, half-heartedly studying the choices of foods on the menu. The Romanian family is already gobbling the pork and hamburgers. The Taverna is crowded with people. Outside the air is hot and the beach looks deserted. The cook moves like a robot, overwhelmed by all the orders. The two waiters perform a dangerous dance between the tables with plates, glasses and bottles.

"You order for me. I'm easy."

"Seafood, octopus, fish?"

"Octopus. I've always wanted to try some and never had a chance."

"Wonderful choice, my friend! Grilled octopus with Greek salad. And two beers."

The waitress nods and goes away without a word. Stelian is left with the feeling that she knows the Greek detective; he even thinks he sees them exchanging meaningful looks, but he doesn't ask. He sighs yet again, thinking of the waves.

"You've really been waiting for this vacation, right?"

"Yes, I have. I wanted to get away from Bucharest and forget it all, work, friends, problems… I wanted to escape somehow. There's a saying about how the end is a new beginning. I didn't really get a chance to enjoy it much."

"I would like to invite you to my house for dinner one night."

"Thank you, but I'm afraid that for the moment I won't be great company. I keep asking myself why did all of this happen?"

"Yes, I keep asking myself the same thing. I just don't see a motive…"

"I was thinking about something earlier. Manole never said anything about a flashlight. He said candles. And it makes sense, I mean two lovers would always pick candles over a flashlight, don't you think?"

"That's right. We'll clarify this right away."

Iannis pulls his cellphone out of his pocket and pushes a button.

"Did you check for fingerprints on all the items found at the crime scene?" he asks in Greek.

"Yes, boss, but most of them are useless."

"What did you find on the flashlight?"

"Nothing. I was going to tell you about this. No fingerprints, plus the glass is broken."

"Thanks."

Iannis hangs up and places the cellphone on the table.

"You were right. No sign of fingerprints on the flashlight and the glass is broken."

"The third party. Maybe a fight. I'm certain there's a third person involved in this."

"Let's not get ahead of ourselves. For now let's just enjoy our meals. Cheers!"

They clink glasses and Munteanu is pleased to find out that Greek beer tastes heavenly. *A bit weird to drink a beer named Mythos, makes you think about something else. But in the end, the name is not important...*

Stelian has managed to momentarily break free from the murder investigation and go to the beach. They have reached a dead end, anyway. The sun is so hot, he can feel it burning even under the enormous umbrella. And he's a bit dizzy—is it from the beer? The sea is calm and filled with kids yelling at each other. He's just finished a long swim, but is still not very happy. He's restless. His phone starts to ring.

"Hello?"

"Mister Munteanu?" In Romanian, an unknown voice.

"That's me."

"My name is Popescu, Daniel Manole's brother-in-law."

"Yes, Mister Popescu. I'm listening."

"I was wondering if we could meet."

Exasperated, Stelian thinks about it for a moment and decides to accept, but not because he wants to meet the guy. The heat has really got to him and he could use a cold drink.

"OK, let's meet. Do you know a place with air conditioning?"

"Hotel Themis. Do you know where it is?"

"I'll find it."

"I'll be in the reception, say in half an hour?"

"Make it forty-five minutes. I need to change."

"Thank you."

Stelian gathers his things, which are now full of sand. *Okay, so the characters start to enter the stage...Popescu is the influential business man. Let's see what he's made of.*

Hotel Themis is just like the rest of the hotels in Paralia. A four floor larger villa that looks like it was built in stages. With every year's profits they've added a new floor. *I wonder if they'll stop at four floors, or keep going up.*

In the reception there's only one man seated in an armchair. He's definitely overweight and is dressed from head to toe in designer sport's clothes: white cotton trousers and polo-shirt. He looks extremely tired and nervous. There's a half-empty glass of something that looks like a café-frappe on the table in front of him and a cigarette is burning in an ashtray. Stelian notices the huge ring with a black stone on the little finger of his left, right next to his wedding ring.

He looks a little ridiculous...I bet he has a black SUV. Mercedes, most likely. Like so many rich people, he doesn't suffer from original-ity...they all look the same.

"Hello, Mister Popescu?" he says aloud.

The man nods his head and extends his hand. A large hand, sweaty, with manicured nails and a very thick gold bracelet. *A hand like a toilet seat*, Stelian remembers from one of his colleagues. He's forcing himself to repress his dislike, even though the man stinks of new money. Money made dishonestly, most likely, right after the '89 Revolution. He shakes Popescu's hand and takes a seat, smothering the impulse to wipe his hand on the tablecloth.

"I'm listening, Mister Popescu."

"Would you like something to drink?"

"Water, please."

Why does he feel the need to seem unlikable? He really wanted an iced coffee and is now being a drama queen. Oh boy, this is going to be one jumpy conversation. The waiter brings his water.

"As far as I understand, Mister Munteanu, you represent the Romanian authorities in this investigation?"

Stelian smiles, almost anticipating the next question.

"Daniel tells me you're a journalist. Why did they send a journalist?"

"As I told your brother-in-law, it's because I was already here. And we don't know yet if Daniel is innocent or not, so bringing a detective from Romania isn't necessary right now. It seems there's another suspect."

"Also Romanian?"

"I can't tell you more. We're still interrogating some witnesses. All we have for now is pure speculation."

"I would like you to leave Daniel alone, Mister Munteanu. The idea that he's a murderer is completely absurd. I'm prepared to do anything to convince you and, of course, the Greek police that he's innocent. Regardless of the costs."

"I'm not sure I understand what you're saying exactly."

"Mister Munteanu, I'm a very rich and influential man."

"I really don't think you can do your brother-in-law any good trying to bribe someone."

"Maybe your words are just a bit harsh, don't you think?"

"I apologize if I misunderstood you. The investigation will continue its course."

"I have a lot of influence, you know. A good word in the right place is always helpful."

"Perhaps a bad one is too."

They stare at each other. Stelian stands up.

"I'm very tired and I think it's better if we end this discussion here. I'll keep you posted with any new developments. As far as the influence goes, I'm not interested. Not right now, anyway. Good-bye!"

He leaves in a bad mood, in search of an iced coffee that he can buy with his own money.

***

Evening again. Stelian had briefly met with Iannis, who had gone home to Katerini. The detective was extremely tired, and he'd had a fight with his wife. She'd been waiting at home with warm food for him for two whole days!

The investigation had reached a dead end: there were clear indications that a third party was involved, but Daniel didn't know anything. He hadn't seen, or heard anything. And the motive was a complete mystery. *If there's a third party in this triangle, the motive could be jealousy.* Tomorrow morning they would go over everything they knew, maybe they were missing something. *If we find the motive, maybe everything will seem more logical. And I can be done with this nightmare!*

Once again, there are a lot of diners at the Poseidon, but he manages to find a table. A small one in a corner close to the street. The waitress—or is it the owner?—recognizes him and, surprisingly, brings him a menu in Romanian. Great! Now all these people know who I am! He orders fish, eggplant salad and a large beer.

"Do you have a light?" asks a man from the nearby table in flawless English.

Stelian turns his head to find a plain looking man dressed in the usual tourist clothing, and wearing a sun hat that is in complete discord with the words he has just uttered. He is also sporting a bright smile.

"Well, do you?"

Stelian searches his pockets—there's always a lighter somewhere, even if he had quit smoking—finds it and offers it to the smiling stranger. He lights a Dunhill from a red package and returns the lighter, his gestures simple, but elegant.

"Thank you! And sorry to have bothered you, I noticed you are quite pensive." He finishes the last drop of the amber coloured liquid in his glass.

"You're welcome. Crazy day."

"May I recommend a Metaxa instead of dessert?" the stranger says, showing his empty glass. "And a good sleep. It clears the mind. So long!"

Stelian looks at him with a curious eye, holding the lighter in one hand and his fork in the other.

Misha Pushkin leaves some money on the table and stands. He quickly disappears in to the crowd, keeping his half-smoked Dunhill close to his chest.

FOUR

THE SUN IS IN HIS EYES. IT'S COOL AND HE CAN HEAR THE noise of the air conditioning in the background. His neck is stiff, but at least he wasn't woken up by another unwelcome phone call. He gets up slowly and looks out the window. The sun is up and the tourists are out in force with their flip-flops. Kids play around the parked cars. It must be really hot outside. He heads to the bathroom and then remembers. For a few moments, he had managed to forgot about the murder investigation. He grimaces in the mirror and wants to go back to bed. Growling, he gives up.

He exercises half heartedly for a few minutes, takes a long shower, then gets dressed and makes his way to breakfast.

"Mister Munteanu, from room 203, right?"

"Yes."

"What would you like to drink, sir?"

The waitress is waiting for his answer, smiling and ready with both a tea kettle and coffee pot.

"Tea, please."

"There you go. I'll be right back. You have a message."

She hurries away and returns with an envelope. A white envelope with no stamp. Stelian butters a piece of toast; he stirs sugar into his tea and takes a sip. He tries to prolong the suspense, but curiosity wins out. The envelope looks ordinary. Someone has written on the back: *To Mr. Stelian Munteanu.* He tears it open. Inside he finds one piece of paper folded in four. There are only three words, which he can't help notice were printed by an inkjet printer: *CHECK THE FUR*. He stares at the words. He had had a feeling from the start that the fur would somehow be important. But check what? At first glance there had been nothing special about it.

"Morning, Iannis."

"Morning, Stelios. Coffee?"

"No, thanks, I had some tea. Maybe later. Any news?"

"Nothing out of the ordinary. We can only assume there was a third person at the crime scene, and that's based on superficial clues: the flashlight with no fingerprints, the imprints of steps found at the Alkion Hotel, the mysterious man seen with the victim a few days prior to the murder."

"Did you get a portrait made of this man?"

"Galia couldn't give us any details. They were too far away, it was evening and people were milling around. All she could say was that there was a man of medium height and build, dressed casually. That's it. It's not enough. They're vague assumptions, nothing definite. He could be anyone from an admirer to a seller."

"You're exaggerating!"

"Obviously. But that's all I have."

"I've got something new. Someone sent me an anonymous letter."

The Greek detective stares at him for a few seconds. Then he extends his hand and, with great care, takes the piece of paper from Stelian. He reads the three words and frowns.

"It has my fingerprints on it. When I opened the envelope I didn't think it would be something related to the murder investigation."

"We'll analyze it at the lab. Very strange, Stelios, like in the movies."

"Someone wants to help us."

"Or put us on the wrong track!"

"I suggest we check the fur one more time. Something tells me that our anonymous friend knows more than we do. And right now we've got nothing to lose. We're at a standstill as it is."

"Agreed."

"One more thing. Invite Galia Kalughina over for another discussion. I've thought of something. It might not be much, but it's worth a try."

The police station is filled with people and maybe that's why it doesn't look as official as it did before. Galia has just arrived, dressed in bright colours, but looking less striking than she did before. She looks better rested, even detached. Conversely, Stelian and Iannis seem worried; both wearing wrinkled clothes and sporting dark shadows under their eyes. Daniel Manole looks exhausted and withdrawn. He's surrounded by a stenographer, a translator and two cops in uniform. On the table there's water and orange juice, white plastic glasses and a tape recorder. The fur coat lies spread over two little tables nearby. The room is silent except for the noise of the air conditioning, working double time to produce a bit of cold. Outside they can hear happy people enjoying their unspoiled vacations.

"Miss Galia, please look at this fur very carefully and tell me if you see something unusual. We found it next to your friend's body."

The woman stands, aware that she's being watched, and approaches the two little tables. Her high heels click like gun shots on the floor. Tension hangs in the air; she seems to understand her importance. She caresses the fur with her fingers unhurriedly.

Stelian sighs impatiently. *Cheap movie tricks. What is she trying to prove? That we depend on her? Shit... this is ridiculous...* He starts to get nervous.

"Please, we're extremely busy," Iannis interjects.

"Of course."

She looks at the fur once more, then turns to face the Greek detective.

"That's not Tania's fur."

There's a sigh of relief, but not from Daniel. It comes from Stelian.

"How can you be so sure?"

"The color is the same, but the cut is different. It's shorter and it has different buttons. Tania's fur had big buttons wrapped in black fabric, this one has metal buckles. I'm certain it's not Tania's fur."

"Could she have bought another one at some point?"

"No, she didn't have the money. And even if she wanted another one, she would have chosen a different color. This one is almost the same color as the first one. Why would someone want two fur coats that look almost the same? It's absurd."

"Are you sure?"

"Absolutely."

"Alright, thank you. Please step into the other room, read your statement one more time and then sign it."

Galia exits, accompanied by the translator and a cop. Again, silence.

"Mister Manole, now it's your turn," the Greek detective addresses the suspect. "Do you have anything to say?"

"I don't know what I could say. Honestly, I can't tell the difference between fur coats. I don't follow fashion. Honestly, I never understood Tania's obsession with this fur. Or the real one...whatever. She wore it everywhere. Except on the beach, of course. She probably dreamed of owning a fur coat for years."

"And why do you think she exchanged it with another?"

"I don't know. It doesn't make sense, since she loved the original so much."

"She never said anything about this fur coat, or the other one?"

"Do you really think we ever talked about fur coats? All I know is that she bought the coat as soon as she got here. That's all I know."

"Mister Manole, you told us that you were planning to run away together."

"Yes, we wanted to go to Paris. She said something about having an aunt there."

"Did she mention an address?"

"No."

"A name?"

"No."

"And how were you planning to make a living? Did you have anything arranged?"

"No. But she said her aunt could help us. And she was planning to sell the fur coat. She thought she could get a good price for it."

"Bingo!" Stelian interjected.

The Greek lieutenant stares at Stelian, who's smiling.

"That's the key. She bought the fur coat in Greece and planned to sell it in Paris. Illegal smuggling!"

Manole stares at him, stunned. Iannis starts to laugh.

"Just an assumption, but, financially speaking, that's not much of a solution. She wouldn't have made much money. These types of deals usually need an intermediary and that means less money for the seller. It's not easy to find a buyer for such an expensive item, especially when you sell it on the black market without a quality certificate. Paris is filled with fur coats. No, this would have been a waste. She would have been better off keeping it."

"Never mind the fact that she cherished it."

"We're missing something. She loved this coat, but at the same time she was leaving for Paris and wanted to sell it. So why did she buy it in the first place? She could have kept the money and gone to Paris."

"Mister Manole, are you holding back any other important details, by chance?"

"No, I don't think so. Nothing that could effect the investigation."

"Good. Nickos, take him into the other room."

The cop exits, followed by Daniel, leaving Iannis and Stelian alone. Iannis pours some coffee in two big cups.

"We're stuck again."

Stelian leans back in the uncomfortable chair and sips the strong coffee.

"In conclusion? It probably wasn't jealousy, or robbery. We're missing something important. There's someone else involved."

"The mystery man?"

"Yes. Imagine this: Tania and Daniel are at the hotel, talking, dreaming, eating ice-cream, smoking, kissing in the candle light. They find themselves without cigarettes and Daniel leaves the scene to buy some. But someone was watching, someone who was already inside the hotel. At exactly the time of the blackout, he makes his way to Tania, a flashlight in hand. He has a discussion with her. They know each other, that's pretty clear, and they know each other well. They argue. Then they share a drink together? Or they don't fight and then it's all premeditated... An accident? The fur coat..."

"Let's make something clear, the accident theory doesn't work. Tania was poisoned and that means the killer was prepared. He had to pour the cyanide in the cognac. He had it ready. Nobody walks around with a dose of cyanide in their pocket, just in case they have to kill someone. They had a drink, like friends. Tania couldn't have suspected anything, since her glass was empty. She drank it all."

"Ok. Tania dies. The killer sees something incriminating about the fur coat, but he can't just take it or it would look like a robbery. So he replaces it."

"But there was no time! Manole was only gone for ten minutes at the most. That can only mean the killer had another fur coat ready. He came with it."

"Well in that case there's only one motive: robbery. The killer wanted that fur coat."

"That's unlikely, Stelios. Nobody kills for a fur coat. At least not in Greece. Besides, why would he switch the furs? They were worth about the same. There was something else about Tania's coat that was worth killing for. But what?"

Iannis shrugs.

"So, where are we?"

"Look, Iannis, this mess is already giving me a headache. Let's take a break. I'll call Bucharest and ask for more details about Tania and her friends. I need to find out more about the nightclub where she danced. Maybe we'll find a lead. I'll ask them to send all the information to your office."

"OK. We'll reconvene around six. If you need a computer, use the one in my office upstairs. I'll run home to Katerini for a little while, before my family forgets what I look like."

"Six o'clock here, then?"

"Yes. Or do you prefer the Poseidon? It's less formal. And people do need to eat sometimes."

"Deal. Six o'clock at the Taverna."

***

Hurrying, Stelian grabs a salad, takes a shower and then crashes into his bed. But his thoughts don't give him peace. Outside the heat is merciless. The air conditioning is whining and he wishes that he'd never left Bucharest. He wonders if he's the unluckiest guy alive. He picks up an Agatha Christie novel from the three books he'd packed for his vacation. The others are more recent, two mass paperbacks by Linda Fairstein and Lisa Scottoline. Crime Scene Collection. Black covers. He never chooses a novel based on the title, but rather its author. This time he had gone for three women. *Somehow, they write better than male writers. Except for Raymond Chandler, the absolute maestro.* The book is thin and he finds a comfortable position, cushioned by the pillows behind his bed. He reads the first lines, but can't concentrate. *The secret rival…*

His cell phone rings and he looks at the screen to see a Romanian number. He answers.

"Stelian, I sent you the information at the number you left. Nothing spectacular. The nightclub is a respectable one. But it seems they have a connection with France. A few girls received invitations for short trips to France."

"Trips? The victim claimed she had an aunt in Paris."

"Well, maybe she was ashamed to say it, but they went there to dance. Maybe some second-rate cabaret. It's difficult to get a dancing job at the famous ones."

"You mean they were signing contracts?"

"We don't have all the details from France. I suspect the owners in Bucharest were trying to find work for the girls over there."

"Work meaning dancing, or something else?"

"Prostitution, you mean? I don't think so. But we'll check just to make sure."

"Thanks a lot, boss. I'll keep in touch."

"Take care."

Despite the cool air in the room, Stelian feels sweaty. He makes his way to the bathroom for another shower. *So, Manole didn't exactly know everything about her. Love isn't so pure and with no strings attached. Not to mention sincerity and trust!*

Iannis had finally made it home, thrown his clothes into the laundry bin and relaxed for an hour in a hot bath, while reading yesterday's newspaper. Then, dressed casually, he returned to the office without having seen a single family member. They had all gone out, but he found little notes from each of them on the kitchen table. They hadn't called, afraid of bothering him. By the time he'll make it home again, they'll all be asleep. Another day without seeing them. He sighs and thinks of retirement. But that's still far off.

He sits at his desk and quickly reads the information received from Bucharest. Most of it is in Romanian, but there's a summary in English.

Daniel Manole has no criminal record. The guy is clean, and Iannis realizes that he's glad. Despite the typical gullible air of a man in love, he likes Daniel. He notices that the Montmartre Nightclub in Bucharest employs only foreign girls. Not a single Romanian! Well, that's the Romanian Police's problem, certainly not his.

He decides to set Daniel free on the condition he doesn't leave town for at least a week. In the meantime, he's sure to find out more about the murder. The killer might lose patience, maybe even make a mistake. At the borders, tourists are carefully screened, especially the Russians and Romanians.

He massages his temples, trying to chase away the pulsating ache. *Why would someone kill for a fur coat? Had she been hiding something there? What kind of information did she possess? And why was it so dangerous?*

He signs the order for Daniel's release and picks up the phone.

"It's Theodopoulos. I signed the release papers. Let him go. I want a list with the surveillance teams on my desk. Don't lose him. Thanks."

He puts the phone back in its cradle. Outside the air is cooler, the sea is peaceful and he wishes he could go swimming. He has some time until six. He walks to the metal closet holding his secret treasures and searches for his swimsuit. He changes.

A nice swim for half an hour in the sea and I'll be as good as new…

FIVE

THE GETTING-READY-TO-GO-OUT RITUAL IS A VERY PLEASANT one for Mikhail, and he follows it to the letter every single chance he gets. *That's what always saved me… my set ways transformed into a routine. The joy to freely and completely enjoy every single moment of loneliness. Another stolen moment from the eternal duty to the country. Especially during the Iron Curtain years.* Now it's a reflex and he feels spoiled whenever he has the chance to do it. He looks at himself in the mirror. He's still relatively young and his mind is as sharp as ever. *That's probably why they kept me on active duty.* He laughs to himself. *They must think I'm easier to control if I'm on their side and not on my own. Which is true. Up to a point.* He smiles and opens his closet, filled with nicely aligned shirts on hangers and four expensive suits ironed to perfection.

He chooses his clothes—warm colors like usual, beige or light blue—and carefully arranges them on the bed. Then the socks and underwear. He shines his shoes, using a special piece of clothing from a plastic bag. A relaxing shower—lavender shower gel, an old Wilkinson razor and the usual Davidoff cologne.

He gets dressed, then checks his pockets: his wallet and passport, together with his fake press credentials—*You never know when you might get caught where you're not supposed to be*—plus a few small euro bills, the rented car keys, his BlackBerry and his handkerchief with the embroidered capital *M* on the corner.

Automatically his hand goes to the spot where his gun holster should be. But it's not there. Just a reflex, since he can't carry a gun here. *The operation is not on yet. I need to wait for a few more details.* His gun remains hidden in a box at the bottom of his suitcase. A 10-mm Glock. A precise and deadly weapon. He smiles, imagining himself in action. He takes out a pack of cigarettes. And leaves his lighter behind on the table...

It's nearly six-thirty in the evening when Mikhail Sergeyevich Pushkin, nicknamed Misha, descends his villa's stairs and starts walking toward the center of town. He'll find the two men somewhere, he's certain of that. *It's time for their secret discussion...*

As usual, the Poseidon Taverna is filled with people. Mikhail's eyes scan all the tables and he mentally congratulates himself. He was right; the two men are seated at a corner table. The trickiest part is how to approach them without raising their suspicions. There's no available table around, and he already used the cigarette trick.

Suddenly a cold shiver runs up his spine. *Damn, I'm not as quick as I used to be. Maybe I should start to consider retirement a little more seriously.* But he knows he's just playing games with himself...

The two men stare at him. One of them, the Romanian, gestures for him to come closer. He can't avoid it any longer and approaches them, composing a *you-talkin'-to-me?* type of expression; neutral.

"Good evening gentlemen, can I help you?"

"Good evening, sir. Are you looking for an empty seat, or a lighter?"

Misha smiles crookedly. *Ha! This little prick is actually making fun of him.* His expression remains very serious and he answers in English, with a heavy British accent.

"Are you inviting me to your table, gentlemen? I wouldn't want to impose."

"Please, sit down."

The Greek detective remains silent, studying him from head to toe. A middle-aged man with hints of grey hair and a medium build. An average guy.

"I really don't want to interrupt. You're probably discussing important matters."

Stelian takes out a cheap plastic lighter from his pocket and places it on the table.

"Please, light your cigarette and let's talk."

It's too late to pull back. Besides, this is exactly what he had been hoping for. He takes out his Dunhills, places one between his lips, lights it, and then passes the lighter back to Stelian.

"Thank you."

"Keep it."

"Thank you again, but I refuse. You might need it sometime. You never know…"

He pauses and straightens his back. *This was easier than I anticipated. These two aren't as amateurish as I thought.* He changes his tone, adopting a more professional one:

"I'd like this conversation to remain off the record. I'm just a simple tourist, even though your superiors, Mr. Theodopoulos, know about my presence here in Paralia."

"Yes, I was told that someone from federal services would show up though I don't exactly understand why. Was the victim collaborating with you?"

"No, far from it. My involvement is for different reasons."

"We're listening."

"Perfect. I won't introduce myself. You actually kind of know me. I was the one who sent the anonymous note, as you probably already realized. But let me get back to the reason why I'm here. It's an old story that goes back fifty years to Siberia, when fragments of diamonds were discovered in the Lena and Vilini Rivers in 1954. That August, the deposits were confirmed and baptized *Tarnita*, which means *Lightning* in Russian. For the next few years, the exploration continued and industrial mining started in ten different areas. However, the climate is brutal. You don't fool around in Siberia, especially when the deposits are located up in the North Arctic Circle. After 1985, there were problems. After 1991, many mines were closed due to lack of equipment and personnel. Government resources were stretched to a breaking point and everything tried up"

"So what? The Mafia stepped in?"

"Yes, as usual at that time. But we're talking diamonds here, not natural gas. Big money from small quantities. There's a huge demand for precious stones in the jewelry shops of France and Switzerland. Can I go on? I hope I'm not boring you. Yesterday's murder represents only the tip of the iceberg."

"We're listening."

"Perfect. During the past few years, illegal smuggling has skyrocketed with the help of all kinds of new technology. The diamond deposits are under continuous surveillance, so it's not easy, but these guys came up with a smart and low risk plan to smuggle the stones into the European Union. Fur coats. Made mostly in Siberia, and I mean made legally. They're processed here, in Kastoria, then sent out to the shops. The girls buy the fur coats here and leave for auditions in France. Once there, they quickly go broke and have to sell their furs. Everything seems above board and absolutely legal. Nothing is left to chance, everything is well planned. And the girls don't suspect a thing."

"Okay, but what does this all have to do with our victim here?"

"Well, this smuggling cartel involves four countries: Russia, Greece, Romania and France. There was a breach. Tatiana found out something and was killed for it. I think she wanted to run away with the diamonds. She betrayed the cartel and was eliminated. That's it, gentlemen."

The cigarette had burned in the ashtray and the beers were now warm.

"I'm sure you must have a lot of questions, but unfortunately I'm not going to answer them. We don't know the number of stolen gems, but we estimate that it's dozens. They're big, most likely over 200 carat, and each coat is probably hiding five or six of them."

"What about the cartel? How many people are we talking?"

"We don't know yet."

"And the fur coat? Were the diamonds hidden in the buttons?"

"Yes, I'm almost certain of it. If the coat was switched, then it means it was hiding something."

"How did you know it was replaced? That's not a known detail."

"I've got my informants, some willing and others not so much…"

"So why are you telling us this?"

"Up until now, we had no real reason to open up the investigation. You can't broadcast that diamonds have been stolen. It's a delicate matter. But, no disrespect to you, we suspect that the person behind this is Romanian. So gentlemen, we'll meet again. I wish you good luck with your investigation. I'll be around…"

Puskin stands.

"One more thing. There is an exceptional crystallography specialist very close by in Salonica. Her name is Eleni Papastergiu."

He nods his head without extending his hand. "Goodbye, gentlemen. We'll see each other again." And disappears.

For a few seconds, time stands still. Iannis recovers first, and calls the waitress.

"Two cups of coffee."

He looks at his watch. Munteanu starts to speak:

"So now that we have a motive, do you think it's too late to contact this Eleni Papastergiu?"

"I don't know. I'll call the office and have them find her. I'll inform Kastoria. Besides, we have to reinforce the borders. We might get lucky."

"If it's not too late already."

The Greek detective massages his temples tiredly.

"We don't even know who we're looking for."

He pays the bill and stands up from the table. Munteanu follows him automatically. The two cups of coffee remain untouched, just like the beers. The waitress stares at them, holding the change. *They'll be back tomorrow…*

The sun is setting, colouring the sky with nuances of orange and purple. On the highway cars start to turn on their headlights. Iannis drives silently, keeping both hands on the wheel. His speed remains a constant 120 km/h on the bluish lit dashboard of the dark blue brand new VW Jetta.

He feels sleepy, but Salonica is close by and he knows they'll get there in no time. He has no idea if Miss Papastergiu will be happy to receive them, but she's been asked help in a police investigation and probably and can't really complain. He pictures her as an old teacher, looking like a grandmother, waiting for them with tea and cakes. *Maybe crocheting warm socks for a hypothetical cold winter, seated under her tired air conditioner.* He smiles without even realizing it…

Iannis parks the car next to the White Tower. During the day, the place is crowded with dozens of tourist buses, but now it's deserted. The city has been invaded by tourists admiring the twinkling ship lights on the horizon. But there's no time join them.

"The building is close by. I know the address."

The eight story building's architecture is quite nice, with elegant modern touches. Large terraces are covered with coloured shades and hanging plants. The elevator stops at the fourth floor and they walk toward an open door. She's been waiting. From behind the door *the granny* welcomes them. Stelian freezes. A tall woman dressed in a simple but elegant dress smiles at them.

"Hello, my name is Eleni Papastergiu. Please, come in."

She's not strikingly beautiful, but carries herself in such a way that it's impossible not to be impressed. Her dress is white, long and very simple. A superb figure. Dark eyes and hair, and white skin. She extends a delicate but firm hand. Stelian melts with every second that passes. Iannis makes the introductions.

"Sit down, gentlemen."

She leads them into a little living room, where they find comfortable and brightly coloured armchairs, and huge windows with a wonderful sea view. One whole wall is covered with bookshelves, a small glass case containing dozens of stones is in one corner. Two marine paintings: fishermen in a storm and a ship returning to a anonymous harbour. Stelian drifts off to his visit to the Soviet Union. *So many years ago. Those were the good times... I was so young. But I've never forgot the art galleries. The Russian Romantics. But this can't be Aivazovsky, maybe some young pupil or some kind of a reproduction.* The room is lit in a warm, intimate way. A cool and welcoming space. Hardly the best spot for questioning. On a glass table there's coffee and appetizers. Stelian quickly erases the image of *the granny* with tea and cakes. He carefully studies the woman again. She's gorgeous.

"How can I help you, gentlemen?"

"It's very late and we've probably ruined your plans for tonight, so I'll get straight to the matter at hand."

"Very well, I'm listening. Please, help yourselves to some coffee and snacks."

"We would like to talk to you about diamonds."

The young woman smiles in amusement. Her white teeth complement her full lips, wearing reddish lipstick.

"I imagined that much."

"You were recommended to us as an exceptional specialist when it comes to Siberian diamonds."

"May I ask by whom?"

"I'm afraid I cannot say."

"I see. It was no secret, anyway. I'm teaching at the University."

"Yes, we know. So, what can you tell us about Siberian diamonds?"

"I've studied the diamond deposits in Russia. As far as I know, however, the mines are now closed. What exactly do you want to know?"

"Well, it seems that the mines are closed only from the government's point of view. The private sector has different ideas. There's a cartel operating on a route that goes from Kastoria, Katerini and Bucharest to Paris. We don't know many details, but the murder we're investigating points us in this direction. In the middle of it all, there's a fur coat supposedly hiding diamonds. Perhaps in its buttons."

"Very ingenious. And original."

"That's what we thought. But is it possible?"

"Were the buttons large enough?"

"About twenty to twenty-five millimetres in diameter. Six pieces, most likely made of plastic."

Stelian suppresses a yawn. The discussion is conducted in proper English. They talk that way for his sake, he knows. He's tired, and the woman in front of him fascinates him. He prefers to keep his mouth shut and just watch. Watch her.

"I've never heard of such methods for hiding diamonds, but I'm not a policeman. Technically speaking, it's possible, although to me it seems like it would be difficult to obtain the stones. Unless the buttons are made of two separate pieces that can be locked together. Kind of like a jewelry box. It would be much simpler."

"Can they be detected by security at the airport?"

"Not necessarily, it depends on the material used for the buttons. A diamond of 150 carats could be placed in the center and would be hard to detect."

"How big is 150 carats exactly?"

"A bit smaller than a cherry seed."

"And what is the value of such a diamond?"

"Depends on its quality, but somewhere close to a few hundred thousand euros."

"So a coat with six buttons could be carrying one to two million euros?"

"Exactly."

Iannis whistles admiringly and sips his coffee.

"I see you're very quiet, Mr. Munteanu."

She looks at Stelian straight in the eyes, still smiling pleasantly. Stelian, prone to post-divorce syndrome, starts to believe in the possibility of love at first sight. He shakes his head, as if trying to clear the fog engulfing his brain.

"I apologize, I find all of this overwhelming. I came here for a nice vacation and hadn't had a chance to rest before being dragged into this investigation."

Iannis feels the uneasiness and takes over.

"As soon as we investigate the fur shops in Paralia and Kastoria we'll send you more information. No doubt we'll need your professional advice."

"What about the Russian police? Did you contact them as well?"

Iannis wonders if the woman knows anything about Misha Pushkin. *Is this a trick question? Are we playing cat and mouse? Who's the cat? Is there only one cat? Who is this lady?*

"No. We don't even have solid proof that the diamonds exist, nor do we have any witnesses, but we have reasons to believe that we're on the right track. We're hoping to find a coat or two in Kastoria, maybe even Paralia."

"I wouldn't be so sure, Mr. Theodopoulos. Regardless of how rich the Tarnita diamond deposits are, it's hard to believe they can uncover so many big stones. If this particular coat contained six diamonds, it'll likely take two or three months before another one shows up. That's my personal opinion, of course, but considering that the mining is illegal, I don't see how they can risk using an army of people for it."

"Yes, you're right. I didn't think of that."

Iannis stands up and Stelian follows him.

"We're leaving now, it's very late. We'll be in touch soon. Once again, please accept our apologies for bothering you on such short notice."

Soon they're back on the street.

"My friend, you're either in love or you have a bad toothache."

Stelian looks toward the sea. He can hear the waves crashing and the calls of the seagulls flying very low.

"At this point, I think I would have preferred a toothache."

The Greek detective starts to laugh. The Romanian becomes even more irritated.

"I'm glad Miss Papastergiu had such an effect on you. We have beautiful women in Greece. But take it easy, my friend. Our women are very picky."

"Thanks for your advice."

"It's late, let's go home."

"Well, some of us can."

"Meaning?"

"Nothing. I think I'm still looking for my place in this world …"

SIX

THE PHONE RINGS. *DAMN! THIS NIGHTMARE IS NEVER ENDING!* He swallows a curse and tries to focus on the sound. It's not his cell phone. It's the room phone.

"Yes," he answers, feeling dizzy.

"Stelios?"

"Yes!"

"Stelios, get up, take a shower and get dressed. I'll be down-stairs in fifteen minutes. Hurry up, will you?"

Stelian lies wearily with the phone in his hand. Nobody has ordered him around like that for a long time. *Since when? The army? My ex-mother-in-law … ex-wife?* But Iannis had sounded extremely worried, so he decides to follow his orders without question.

It's still early in the morning and the air feels cool. He finds the Greek detective waiting for him in the hotel's reception. His clothes are wrinkled and his eyes are puffy. He's visibly agitated. They quickly shake hands.

"Let's go to the car. I'll explain everything on the way. We're going to Katerini, to our main office. We have all the necessary equipment over there."

Iannis drives his car very carefully; he seems nervous. He looks straight ahead. The driver's window is open and the strong gust of air makes both of them more alert.

"Sorry for ordering you around. I was rude. I got carried away."

"No problem. You must have your reasons."

"I'm very worried …"

"What happened?"

"Everybody's disappeared."

"Everybody, who?"

"Everybody! Daniel Manole and the Popescu couple, Galia, the victim's friend, even Pushkin, the Russian guy."

"Where did they disappear to?"

"If I knew the answer to that question, I wouldn't be so stressed!"

"Sorry, stupid question."

"No need to apologize."

"And how did you find out?"

"I sent one of my colleagues to invite the three Romanians for a last chat. I thought that maybe we could sort out the details, but they weren't at their hotel anymore. The receptionist over at the Themis Hotel informed me that the Romanians had paid for their rooms late last night, filled their car with suitcases and left right after midnight. He had no idea about their destination. Then I wanted to talk to Galia about the victim and the nightclub in Bucharest, but it seems she left for a party and never returned to her hotel. She must have tricked my men."

"Do you think she wanted to escape surveillance? Or just wanted to have some fun?"

"I don't know, but I have no idea where she is right now."

"It's still early, maybe she'll show up."

"I hope so. I'm worried. She didn't take any luggage and she hasn't changed her clothes. The room is paid for. Was she kidnapped, or did she simply run away?"

"I don't see any reason why she would run."

"Me neither. I hope we don't end up with a second victim on our hands."

"God forbid, but Galia doesn't have a fur coat, so I don't see a motive."

"Maybe the killer thinks she knows too much. If he panics he could be capable of anything."

"What about the borders?"

"I don't know. I tried to block all the exits, but I couldn't cover them all. I can't get a warrant. There's no legal basis. Not yet."

"What about the Russian guy?"

"He was the best. He sent me an email: *I'm leaving. Urgent matters. I'll be in touch as soon as I can. See you soon. Mikhail Sergeyevich Pushkin.*"

"And he's gone?"

"That's right. I don't even know how he knew my email address."

"Well, it's not like it's top secret. And I'm sure he has contacts."

"Wonderful. Now we're all alone with no suspect."

"Were you suspecting Pushkin of anything?"

"I verified him on our network. Interpol's too. He has a great cover as a journalist and adviser in external affairs. He works all around Europe and speaks six languages fluently. Couldn't find out much about him. My access was limited. He could be anyone."

"Even an illegal dealer and murderer?"

"I won't assume anything. Anyways, we don't have anything on him. Maybe he was called back to Russia, maybe he gave up on this particular investigation."

"I doubt it, Iannis. Believe me, an ex-KGB op doesn't give up so easily. He's somewhere around and will show up when we least expect it."

The car drives in to Katerini. The traffic is heavy in the small city so Iannis starts his siren and flashing lights. Stelian thinks the siren sounds like a mourning song.

The boat approaches the shore. The sun is beating down relentlessly. No cloud over the horizon. The harbour is deserted. The island of Skiathos is still asleep. The small boat doesn't attract unwanted attention. Called the *Thalia,* it sails under a Greek flag and is registered in Piraeus. With the paint peeling, and the engine purring tiredly, it certainly isn't new. In the wheelhouse cabin, which sports a cracked window and an old poster serving as a sunshade, there's a single man at the helm.

Mikhail Sergeyevich Pushkin crushes yet another spent Dunhill into the overfilled ashtray and prepares to dock. *It'll be even more difficult to take her ashore than it was to convince her to board the boat. She'll be asleep for a few more hours, anyway. I'll have to find a way to not make it look suspicious. As long as I don't run into anyone too curious...*

In the comfortable cabin below, elegantly dressed but with her hair a complete mess and without her sandals, Galia sleeps heavily. It's not her fault, though. The sleeping pills was very powerful.

***

There are few people at the Katerini communication centre and it's quiet. Iannis sits in front of a computer, his hands flying over the keyboard. Stelian is outside in the hallway, enjoying a sandwich and a cup of weak coffee. There's little reason for him to be inside since he doesn't speak a word of Greek.

Iannis finally connects the audio-video network to a border agent.

"Any problems last night?"

"None of the missing persons showed up at the borders."

"Did you keep an eye on the airports too?"

"Of course."

"What about on the sea?"

"The usual traffic. Nobody crossed into international waters."

"Cruise ships?"

"None that have left yet. But we had two arrivals, one to Salonica, one to—"

"Not interested. What about private boats?"

"Only in our waters."

"Nothing suspicious?"

"No. Well, maybe just one..."

"I'm listening."

"*Clochard*, registered in Nice. Exited the harbour at three this morning. That's a bit early, even for fishing."

"Who's on board?"

"We don't know. The control point only registered the exit."

"Who's the owner?"

"A French man. Jacques Colbert."

"Which harbour did he leave from?"

"Halkidiki, from Akti Sani."

"Can we follow him on radar?"

"Of course. Do you want us to stop him?"

"Not yet. We don't know who's on board and we don't want to make any mistakes. Follow him and inform me if he approaches another boat."

"Are we looking for something specific?"

"No. Unfortunately, I don't even know what we're looking for."

"The boat is still in our territorial waters. Doesn't look like it's in a hurry. Speed is constant at sixteen knots. Going south. We can keep an eye on him for another eight hours. What do we do?"

"Nothing. Just keep a discreet eye on him. I'll let you know as soon as I find out more."

"Understood."

Iannis exits the room and almost crashes into Stelian, who was pacing the hallway with a bored expression.

"Found anything?"

"I don't know. A French boat sailed out of Hakidiki a few hours ago. Nothing at the borders."

"They must be hiding somewhere."

"I don't get it. Why did they disappear? All of them."

Munteanu shrugs. *I'm out of my league. No matter how much I try to play the great detective, I know nothing about police investigations. Even though I worked as a journalist, it doesn't mean that...*

The door opens suddenly and a young man talks hurriedly:

"Sir, we have something."

Theodopoulos disappears inside. He's back in less than a minute.

"It's them!"

"Who?"

"The Popescu couple and Daniel Manole. We got a visual when they passed a coastguard boat. The images were scanned and compared with their pictures. I'm sure it's them."

"How did you get their pictures?"

"From their IDs. I asked Bucharest for copies and received them right away."

"Wow! That's incredible! I didn't know that was possible."

"A lot of things are possible with this new technology. It's people who are the real problem."

"I gather you guys have the same kind of problems we have?"

"It's the Balkan curse."

"So, did they stop them?"

"No. For now I want to let them believe they've gone unnoticed."

"You'll allow them to leave the country?"

"If only I knew where they're headed... But for now I think it's better if we follow them at a distance."

"Any news about the others?"

"No. I hope they're somewhere in Greece. Pushkin is a pro, he knows how to go dark. Galia's the problem. We'll wait until tonight, and if she doesn't show up then I'll put her on the wanted list. But I still don't have any solid evidence. It's getting more and more difficult... and to top it all off, we're in tourist season."

The *Clochard* boat is new and kitted out with all kinds of gadgets. An expensive white machine—special-ordered in less than six months—it is fitted with high-powered engines, stainless steel rails and tinted windows. A poor man's dream, but standard issue for the wealthy.

And there is no doubt that Popescu is rich. He passes a hand over his face and pulls down his sun hat, irritated by the strong sun. He looks straight ahead with his steely grey-blue eyes; his face is cold, unreadable.

A luxurious way to get around on vacation and a quick mode of escape in an emergency. Without this boat there was no way I could have rescued Daniel from the Greek police.

Relaxed, he steers the boat with finesse and skill. The sea calms him down. Open spaces. Freedom. He has had a master's certificate for almost twenty years now; he earned during the Communist regime. He'd scared the shit out of Daniel and Nora with this hurried departure, but he had to try to safely take them out of the country. He was certain they would have been stopped at any border, including the airports. He had spoken with his lawyer on the phone. Daniel could be detained at any moment for 24, or even 48 hours to give more statements. Taking him out of the country was the only viable solution. And, since he was the head of the family, it was his responsibility.

His thoughts end quickly with a shudder. Too late. The coastguard boat is close. Too close. Lost in thought, he'd neglected to pay attention to the radar announcing the arrival of another boat. *That's what I get for daydreaming and not paying attention.* Now I pay for it. Like I do for every little moment of joy. He has no time to warn Daniel and Nora sunbathing at the stern. The tiny glitter of binoculars from the coastguard boat confirms that they've been spotted. *Since they're playing cat and mouse, it's obvious they have no idea who they're looking for. By the time they decide, I'll be far away. Daniel is in good hands.*

The heat is unmerciful, it almost feels like a heavy weight on your body. It's hard to breathe. Even the weak breeze burns everything in its way. The shades are down, the air conditioning are on full blast, the streets are empty and terraces deserted. Nothing moves in the harbour. Well, almost nothing.

A motorcycle with a sidecar is being lowered from an old Greek fishing boat docked at the end of the pier, accompanied by the wailing of a World War II-era crane. The motorcycle is also old, a 1970 Russian IJ, sloppily painted in ugly dark color. Inside the sidecar someone with a white hat pulled over their eyes is soundly asleep. The mysterious character remains asleep even when the motorcycle reaches the ground and settles with a jolt. A man dressed in fisherman clothes, stained with oil and grease, mounts the motorcycle and starts the engine. It coughs a few times before starting with a roar.

The Skiathos streets are tiny, a remnant of the city's Venetian past. Laundry is hanging out to dry overhead, red Geraniums spilling from countless flower pots. The old motorcycle engine makes an infernal noise. Pushkin is stressed, sweating profusely under his fake moustache. But the uphill road is not too long and he arrives at the white safehouse on top of the hill without problem. The wooden shades are closed and the house looks deserted. Galia, hat pulled over her eyes, is still asleep.

Misha opens the gate and drives the motorcycle through. He unlocks the entrance door, then lifts Galia with a grunt. He places her on a couch in the house. After quickly hiding the motorcycle under a discoloured tarpaulin, he returns to the house and locks the door.

The interior looks just as old and abandoned as outside, but a huge, new fridge purrs silently in the kitchen. Next to it sits a microwave and stove. The living room sports a fancy new stereo. It's a weird mix of old-fashioned and all-mod-cons. The air conditioning keeps the temperature at a pleasant 18 degrees Celsius.

Misha returns to Galia and places a pillow under her head. He removes a bottle of South African Riesling from the fridge. The bottle is cold and fogs instantly. He removes an old-looking bottle opener from a drawer and finds a crystal glass hidden in a cabinet. Before opening the bottle he brings a bag containing a laptop in from the living room. He pours the wine slowly, waiting for the laptop to fire up. A small window opens. He types with one hand, holding the wine glass with the other.

I need a transfer. Skiathos. 7 hours. Confirm.

He pours more wine and starts to relax.

From the helicopter, Stelian is given a magnificent view of the Greek islands.

"They have three choices: Crete, Cyprus, or Malta. But Crete is ours, so what's left is…"

The engine starts loudly. The helicopter is a four-seater Bell belonging to the coast guard. Stelian and Iannis are seated right behind the pilots. Iannis gestures for Stelian to put on the headphones, then continues:

"I was saying that most likely they'll choose Malta or Cyprus."

Munteanu automatically approves with a nod. He doesn't entirely understand what's going on, but he's not up for conversation. The helicopter ride is an interesting experience, even if this frantic chase doesn't make any sense to him. *We could just follow them on the radar. Why all this craziness?*

"What do you think they're trying to do?"

"They want to hide."

"What proof do you have?"

"I don't know exactly. But it's clear that they want to escape Greece. Where do they go from here…"

"I think they want to go back to Romania. They know we have no solid proof against Manole. Popescu is rich and he has a lot of connections back there, so he can protect Manol."

"Yes, that's one option. I just want to make sure."

Stelian leaves it at that. Galia's disappearance, and especially Pushkin's, worries him the most. *Who can guarantee that Pushkin doesn't operate his own illegal cartel? After all, he's Russian, has access to information and moves quickly. It's quite possible that he's playing two sides.*

The helicopter flies over the sea. The view is superb, the sky is clear, the visibility perfect.

"Mr. Theodopoulos, *Clochard* changed course. They're sailing north now."

"North?! Why the hell are they going back? Even if they suspect we're following them, I don't get it…"

"I really don't know who's chasing who," Munteanu comments. "I've got an idea. Can you connect me to this number in Bucharest?"

Iannis talks to the pilots.

"You're connected. Place the call, it's working."

"Thanks."

The phone rings twice, then a female voice answers in Romanian:

"You have reached Tarom, the Reservation Service. How may I help you?"

"Hello. Munteanu speaking. May I speak to Delia?"

"Right away. One moment, please."

Munteanu smiles and winks at Iannis. The helicopter has changed course, but it's still flying high.

"Yes?"

"Hi, Delia. Stelian Munteanu here. Is this a bad time?"

"Not at all! What a surprise! Haven't heard from you in a while. What's going on?"

"Well, you won't believe this, but I'm in a helicopter, flying over the Aegean Sea and… Well, I really don't have time to explain but I'll take you out for a coffee when I get back."

"Yeah, right. That's what you always say and never keep your promise."

"I will this time!"

"We'll see about that. What do you need?"

"Three passengers: Nora and Mircea Popescu, and Daniel Manole. They should show up on a flight to Bucharest tonight."

"There are many Romanians named Popescu."

"They should have seats together…"

"Yes, I've found them. The flight from Rome, reservation made straight from Bucharest less than an hour ago. By phone, not online. They were either lucky or had good connections to get seats at such short notice."

"Oh, yeah, they've got big connections. Thanks a lot. I'll call you when I get back."

Stelian ends the call and thanks the pilots.

"I'm listening, Stelios."

"I think I know what they intend to do. Can you find out where's the nearest international airport with flights to Rome?"

"Rome? Let me check."

Iannis makes a few calls. Munteanu can't understand a word of it, so he takes the opportunity to watch the scenery. The sea is blue and peaceful. The islands are an exotic mix of rocks, green and white sandy beaches. The boats like white drops on the blue water.

"Skiathos International. The *Olympic* flight, departing at 14:45. Now, what's the catch?"

"They're taking a roundabout route. Boat to Skiathos, flight to Rome for a cup of coffee, and then a quick Tarom flight to Bucharest. Zigging and zagging, like they're dodging gunfire. Stupid, but efficient."

"If you say so. Let's go to Skiathos, then. We'll get them there."

SEVEN

THE AFTERNOON BRINGS WITH IT SOME COOLER AIR. NOT much, but enough for the little taverna's owners to show their sleepy faces again, holding tall café frappe glasses. The first customers start to arrive. Seated at a table under a multicoloured umbrella, Pushkin watches through his binoculars as an unexpected boat prepares to dock. His worry grows with every minute that passes. He recognizes the shape of the boat. Then he reads the name: *Clochard.* He hadn't expected visitors. *Especially these visitors!*

Suddenly there's a loud noise and a coast guard helicopter appears from behind the few anaemic clouds, crossing the little gulf to come inland at low altitude. The air current leaves small waves behind, gently rocking the boats docked in the harbour. Irritated seagulls fly in all directions. The customers seated at the tables don't take any notice.

They'll be landing at the airport. The police finally got it. This place has become too crowded. Is this the last dance? A coincidence, or an organized operation?

Pushkin leaves a few euros on the table, swallows the last of his already warm beer, and sets off down the maze of narrow streets.

The two men are seated in a corner at a bar right next to the departure gate. The armchairs are green and very comfortable. Two untouched black coffees cool on the round, stainless steel table.

"I really don't understand this foolish sea chase. Are they making fun of us, or do they really have a reason for all this?"

"Hard to say for now. But I don't think so."

"But they must know we'll get them eventually."

"Probably, but they also know we don't have any proof against them. Someones trying to stall for time. But for what…"

"Okay Iannis, let's sum it up. We have a young Russian woman, Tatiana Sevcenko, killed because she knew too much; a fur coat hiding diamonds in its buttons, which is most likely in the killer's possession; and a bunch of suspects. Daniel Manole is back on the list and now we can add the Popescus…"

"You think they're accomplices?" Iannis asks wistfully.

"They were together on that boat. We'll have to see. Then there's Tatiana's girlfriend, Galia, who's missing. Was she kidnapped, or did she run away?"

"I suspect she's been kidnapped. She's key. Surely she knows more than what she let on. We're doing everything in our power to find her."

"Then there's Pushkin. The mysterious adviser. I would put him on the top of our suspect list."

"It's not likely. We have strong indications that he's a pro playing on our side. My personal favourite remains Daniel Manole. That could only mean that the third missing person that night..."

"It could be Pushkin!"

"No. Even if he's playing a double game, he's not a killer."

"They could be accomplices, Pushkin and Manole."

"And the two Popescus? We don't know anything about the wife. It looks too much like an international conspiracy."

An overhead voice announces the boarding of a flight.

"That's your flight, Stelios. Keep an eye on them. We'll keep in touch. Everything is set for your transfer in Rome. Good luck."

They shake hands like brothers, but the gesture seems a bit pathetic. Munteanu feels ridiculous, but he's too tired to control himself. He mumbles a curse and then remains quiet. Then he realizes he doesn't have any luggage. His suitcase is back at the Elektra Beach Hotel. He doesn't say anything. He knows the Greek police will send it to him. Somewhere. Perhaps to Bucharest. He waves and disappears through the gate.

Fiumicino Airport is crowded and hot. Smoking is forbidden, but the air is filled with the smell of fast food, sweaty clothing and expensive perfume. The continuous chatter and humidity make for a disconcerting air. Munteanu fidgets in his chair, trying to find a comfortable position for a quick nap.

"Well this is a real surprise, Mr. Policeman."

He straightens up. *Surprise my ass! I wasn't even trying to hide!* He'd known they would show up, but hadn't expected them to confront him. Mircea Popescu stares at him without extending his hand.

"You decided to cut short your busy vacation for a stop-over in Rome on your way home?"

Munteanu doesn't feel like joking, so he merely stares back and says:

"Actually, I was following you."

Popescu hadn't expected such a straight answer and remains quiet. Stelian notices his two companions seated a few seats away. They remain silent, staring at him. Time to take the upper-hand.

"We didn't want to interfere with your short sea escapade so we kept our distance. However, now I've got nowhere to hide. This waiting room is a bit small."

"Am I to understand that we should expect a welcoming committee in Bucharest?"

"You know better than that. Didn't you say that you're highly connected?"

"Mr. Munteanu, it would be a pity to go on like this. Maybe we can forget what's happened in Skiathos and we could start over."

"It's not my fault our relationship is what its is, Mr. Popescu. And honestly, we've got nothing in common. I can't imagine what we could talk about. We're from completely different worlds, we have different values ."

"As you wish."

Popescu turns around and joins his wife and brother-in-law. Stelian is a wreck. The fatigue and stress from the last few days really annoys him. Maybe he shouldn't have been so brutally honest. *Why did all of this have to happen to me? Am I that unlucky? Why couldn't I enjoy a nice, peaceful vacation? No worries. No running around. No bosses breathing down my neck.* Once they land in Bucharest he'll be done with this investigation. They'll find some smart detective to take over.

Drifting off, he pictures the waves in Paralia and the face of that beautiful Greek woman, Eleni. The coloured armchairs, the blue sea, her eyes and hair, her full lips...

"Passengers flying to Bucharest are invited to board at gate fourteen."

Stelian mumbles a curse as he stands. He had fallen asleep.

At Bucharest's Henri Coandă Airport, inside the new arrivals ter-
minal, Toni Demetriade tosses his gum in the metal trash can. It
wouldn't be polite. Besides, it had lost its taste ages ago. He's dressed
in civilian clothes: a green, short-sleeved shirt and dark green, linen
trousers, a light khaki jacket hiding the gun at his waist. It's habit,
and he doesn't expect he'll need it. He has an idea of what Munteanu
looks like, so he hasn't brought a sign with his name.

The flight from Rome has landed and the passengers start to
pour out. The man he's waiting for appears, looking sweaty and a
bit lost, carrying a plastic bag on his shoulder.

"Mister Munteanu?"

"That's me."

"I'm Inspector Demetriade."

They shake hands. The young policeman smiles professionally.

"Nice to meet you. Do you have a car?"

"Obviously."

The reply jolts Stelian, and he wants to fire back with an ironic
response. Instead, he coldly glares and then manages to calm
himself down. After all, this smart ass cop hasn't been chasing
potential murderers across the Mediterranean.

"Glad to hear it."

"Let's go, then."

"I'll follow you."

"You don't have any luggage?"

"No, I left my luggage back at my hotel in Greece."

Toni stays silent, sensing the high level of irritation, and doesn't
push things further.

In the parking lot, Stelian spot the Popescus leaving in a sleek
black BMW X5. Of course, they have a chauffeur. Mircea Popescu
waves ironically. Stelian get into an old Dacia 1310, slamming the
door before putting on his seat belt. He rolls down the window.

"So, I guess I wasn't worth a newer, air conditioned car?"

"Sorry, I couldn't get you a Logan."

"Great, now I really feel like I'm back home."

"Maybe this isn't the right time, but I have news for you. Some good some bad."

Stelian watches Demetriade as he stops and starts the old car in heavy traffic. The road in to Bucharest is very busy.

"Glad to know good news still exists. Start with the good news."

"Those days you've been to Paralia won't be considered vacation days."

"Wonderful. And the bad news? There's a price for everything."

"The bad news is that you're still on this case. I was named as your assistant. The big boss said he'll personally send you away on vacation when all this is over. For as long as a month."

"Yeah, I've heard that before."

"I figured you won't be too pleased, so I thought you should know about it right away."

"Don't you think I'm unqualified to investigate a murder?"

"That's exactly why we'll be working together."

Munteanu sighs heavily.

"Okay. If we're a team let's cut the crap. You can call me Stelian."

"I'm Toni. What time do you want me to pick you up tomorrow morning? Nine thirty sound good?"

"Perfect."

They remain silent for the rest of the drive. Bucharest seems more peaceful in darkness. The mix of street lights, headlights and brightly lit billboards, create a fuzzy glow. Stelian feels himself slipping off into sleep again.

EIGHT

IT'S MORNING AND IT'S QUIET. SO QUIET THAT YOU CAN HEAR the neighbour's fridge humming and the crying baby five floors down. Fragments of noise filter up from the street: a honking car, fragments of a passing conversation and a barking dog. For once, there's no phone ringing. Munteanu gets out of bed almost feeling happy.

His apartment is very small. Two rooms, with little comfort. *One room and three quarters, more like it.* Seventh floor. The building was built around 1970, with eight single and double-room flats on each of the eleven floors, spread over three wings. A lot of old people, most of them retired and poor. *Ceausescu's invented city dwellers, who used to stand in huge lines for days in order to buy tiny chickens and milk in plastic bags. There's no lines now, but no more jobs either. No money!*

He walks from the bathroom, with its thirty-year-old tiles, through the tiny kitchen into his small bedroom which consists of white walls and a fold-out sofa. He has to pack it up every time he has company, at least trying to pretend there's a bit more space. The drowsiness lurking in his body tempts him to get back into bed.

What the hell is wrong with my life? Images flash through his head like a silent movie…his four-year-old daughter, Lulu, smiling innocently. She's out of the country now, living with her mom. Happy moments mix with memories of lost battles. His unsatisfying work. *I've always been a rebel. Working for the government kills me.* The publishing house he abandoned. The stories and dreams behind every book published. His projects. He stares at his image reflected in the mirror and sighs. *Okay, let's put everything in order. The investigation. Eleni? My resignation…sooner or later I'll have to do it. What's next? Editor again? Journalist? Stop!*

He jumps back to his feet and has a quick cold shower. There's ironed clothing in his closet. *Thank God Mrs. Gica came by while I was gone!* He picks out a classic grey suit. Outside, he can see the signs it will be a hot and dusty day. *I'll sweat like a pig in that damn car!* He eats two ham and cheese sandwiches and drinks his strong, bitter coffee. He's ready now. He looks at his watch: twenty past nine. *Perfect!*

Standing in the front of his building are two old retired men dressed in holding empty bags and lamenting the cost of living. He waves and receives the usual response: *All the best, neighbour!* Toni Demetriade stands next to the Dacia that in daylight seems even older.

"Morning, sleep well?"

"Yes, but not enough. You couldn't find a real car?"

"Nope, this was the only one available. Besides, we're undercover."

"This is undercover? Whatever, where to?"

"We'll go see the big boss."

They get in the car and Demetriade pulls out a package from the dashboard.

"I think you could use this," he says as he hands him a Beretta pistol in a leather holder.

"That's stupid. I can't carry a gun, Toni, I'm not even a policeman."

"Sorry, orders from up high. You're not on vacation anymore and a lot of things can happen around here. Better safe than sorry. We don't want any surprises, especially after this shady mess."

Munteanu shrugs.

"Well, if I'm to obey the orders…"

"Don't waste your breath, just take it" Toni interrupts him, but then shuts up, realizing that he's overreacted. *Damn me and my big mouth.*

Stelian thinks again about retirement. *Not now. Later! Wait, the time will come…* He slides the gun holster through his belt and removes the gun to feel it in his hand.

"It's got a nice feel. I was pretty good at target shooting in high school."

"I know, I've read your file."

"Ha, good one. What are you, the ex-Securitate?!"

Demetriade laughs half heartedly.

"I had to read it if we're going to be a team. Forget that though, let's talk what we need to do."

"Sorry, ignore me, I get down easily these days. I'm listening."

The car exits between two buildings and turns onto Şoseaua Pantelimon, passes a hospital and Demetriade accelerates.

"The Popescus moved quickly. Their lawyers are like bulldogs, we can't touch them. As for the Montmartre nightclub, we can't get anything on it. There's no watered down booze or rotten food, they're clean. But, here's a real bomb for you: Galia Kalughina show up in Romania last night."

"How did she get back? What border did she use?"

"Ruse. They didn't stop her."

"What about the disappearance act she pulled in Greece?"

"I got the story."

"What did she say?"

"Her story was pretty childish. She went to a yacht party and fell asleep. She woke up on the Bulgarian coastline, over in Zlatni Pyasatsi."

"What's that?"

"The Golden Sands, a very trendy seaside resort these days. The place is swarming with Romanians, Russians and Germans. It's kind of like Mamaia here, just on the north side of Varna."

"Well it's obviously a lie. And from there?"

"The Montmartre sent a car for her. She had a room under her name at the Berlin Golden Beach Hotel. Paid for two nights."

"Unbelievable. This is like in a bad movie. She say anything else?"

"Yes, that she doesn't remember anything else."

"Wonderful. What the hell is going on? Something is missing. Nothing makes sense."

Toni remains silent. The traffic is quite heavy. The tram lines are getting replaced on the Ştefan cel Mare Boulevard and the underground passages are closed off.

When they finally arrive at the station, they're out of luck. The Chief Inspector Asaftei was called to an emergency meeting over at the Ministry.

"And now what, Toni?'

"We can visit a park or a museum."

"I'm not in the mood for jokes!"

"How about a coffee?"

"That sounds better."

Despite the heat, the center of Bucharest is abuzz. They head to a pizza place across the street from the Boulevard Hotel. *This once used to be Delta Dunării*, remembers Stelian. *Lines stretched for kilometers for a bit of fresh fish. People were sick of tinned sardines in tomato sauce.*

It's a good spot, with few customers and, most importantly, an air conditioning that works.

"I feel like I never want to leave this place. Let's order."

"The only thing I want right now is a cappuccino, Toni."

"Me too."

The waiter retreats without a word after taking their orders.

"So, what can we figure out while we wait to meet with the big boss?"

"I got some information about the Popescu family."

Toni removes a bunch of folded papers from his breast pocket.

"There's a brief about each of them. Do you want to read them now?"

"No. You can sum it up for me. What's Popescu up to?"

"We only know the tip of the iceberg. He owns quite a few export-import companies, primarily in the printing business: ink, paper, different second-hand printing equipment from France. He brings paper in the country from Slovakia and Chișinău ..."

"Chișinău?"

"Yeah, he's actually there right now. He took a flight out this morning."

"Quite a sudden departure, don't you think?"

"We had no reason to stop him and Daniel Manole is still here."

"What else?"

"He represents some ink manufacturers from Germany and owns a mid-sized French-Romanian tourist business."

"What about the yacht he used in Greece?"

"It belongs to the owner of the Montmartre, Jacques Colbert."

"So they know each other."

"Absolutely. We even suspect they're in business together. Regardless, Popescu has super high connections. He's well protected. I was warned not to make too many waves until we get something concrete. He's quite protective of his family and will stop at nothing if we step on his toes."

"Yeah, I got that over in Paralia. He offered me things, and when I refused, he openly threatened me. I can't stand him."

"Nobody like this guy. But he's very dangerous. But we've got nothing on him."

"What throws me off a bit is his wife, Nora. I've met him and Daniel, but never spoke to the wife. She's inaccessible."

"It might be her choice, or the silence could be forced."

Toni searches through the papers and then reads aloud:

"Nora Popescu, maiden name Manole. Thirty-five years old. Graduated from the Bucharest University with a law degree, specializing in community law in Paris and Hanover. Member of the Bucharest Lawyers Association. She married Popescu nine years ago and had been working as a lawyer up until five years ago, when she suddenly closed her business."

"And so she's a housewife."

"Looks that way."

"Any kids?"

"No. There's a story somewhere about a miscarriage that left her sterile, or something like that."

"Was that when she gave up on her career?"

"Probably not. This marriage looks too much like a contract to me."

"In what way?"

"The Manole family is poor and Popescu stepped in. They're not even from Bucharest, they're from Alexandria. Small city, no jobs, no money."

"Popescu wanted a young and beautiful wife so he bought her from the countryside?"

"That's a bit brutal, Stelian."

"But I'm right."

He lights a cigarette, and only inhales twice before he crushes it in the ashtray. *I really have to quit!*

"I have one other question. What did Mircea Popescu do before 1989?"

"He worked for a pulp and paper factory that was attached to the Ministry of Forestry and Construction. He was a supervisor, then promoted to Deputy Director."

"Classic. Then he used his connections to start his business."

"There are certain rumours about him financing a certain political party. One that makes a lot of noise to attract people."

"Well Toni, if you're relying on rumours we're screwed."

They both laugh.

"And who runs the nightclub?"

"Well. that's the surprise for you tonight. Ionel Pavel, the head of the Montmartre is going to meet us tonight at nine-thirty. We'll have a little drink and talk about his nightclub and its girls."

"Nightclub and girls? I could think of worse things."

"Yeah, one the small, but infrequent, perks in our work."

"Unfortunately, he's ready for us, so we can't take him by surprise."

"He's already been told that we're coming to meet him."

"Very interesting connections. Popescu has businesses in France. His partner has a nightclub in Bucharest. His brother-in-law falls in love with a dancer from this nightclub while in Paralia. Although he's never met her before they decide to run away to France. All this stinks, don't you think?"

"Yeah, it stinks. Maybe Daniel Manole isn't a fan of nightclubs."

"Sure, he reclusive like his sister, who suddenly became a housewife after a sensational career."

"Well, what do you think this is all about?"

"Could be just foolishness, some kind of an advantage, or simply blackmail. But I doubt it was foolishness so we're left with the other two. Where can we find Nora Popescu?"

"I have her address in Băneasa. Mircea is still in Chişinău and Daniel lives in Bucharest. She's probably home alone. It's still early. Should I give her a call?"

"I think a surprise visit is a better idea."

"OK. Let's go."

A white Opel Astra Caravan carefully snakes through the twisted road descending from Poiana Braşov to Braşov. Covered in dirt and mud, it has seen better days. The road is clear. Misha Pushkin feels tired and annoyed. He tried to put a few clues together, visited two different people, but has no results to show for it. For now.

There's a sudden crack in the windshield which quickly blossoms. He is no stranger to the noise and immediately recognizes the danger. There's no other cars in sight. In seconds he accelerates. He's not going to take unnecessary risks; the attacker is well hidden and the second bullet won't miss. His right hand leaves the stick shift and retrieves the 10 mm Glock from the glovebox. His hands leave the wheel for a second to arm the gun and then he places it on the passenger's seat. Fortunately, he is cautious. The attacker is either not a pro or in a hurry, but he doesn't suspect that's the case. Most likely the gun was a small calibre used from too far away. It's quiet again. The road is deserted.

Finally, he reaches the Aro Palace Hotel. He parks and places the gun in the underarm holster. *Better safe than sorry!* He looks around and enters the bar. A nice vodka will calm him down. He hadn't anticipated the attack. *A warning, or a failed operation?* Or simply the stress of the situation causing his adversary to make mistakes? *Just like chess, I'll be waiting for him to slip up.*

NINE

THE IMPRESSIVE VILLA HAS TWO FLOORS AND A TILED ROOF, but doesn't strike him as overly opulent. It sits back behind a high fence. Pipera became the city of the nouveau riche after the Revolution. These fenced communities are the new Berlin walls. *The ones built under capitalism. Brrrr ... I'm starting to get nostalgic for the old communist regime, me the big liberal.*

The car stops in front of the metal gate. There's a surveillance camera and an intercom. Stelian gets out and presses the green button. *They should have bought the ones you can reach from the car, like in the American movies.*

"Yes?"

"Hello, my name is Stelian Munteanu, I'm with the police. I met your husband in Paralia. I would like to talk to you about your brother, Daniel. I'm in charge of the investigation."

"I'm not Mrs. Popescu. Please wait for a moment while I tell her."

Munteanu wipes his sweaty forehead. The sun is overhead now. *No surprise. They have a maid.* He feels like he's in a bad movie. He almost gives up when the big gate starts to swing open.

The garden is immense. They park on the left side of the villa, under a few young apple trees. The road is paved with colourful, hexagonal stones. Fruit trees and rose bushes are everywhere, nice garden lamps completing the tasteful design. Nothing out of place, everything refined and elegant. The villa is white with no unnecessary accessories. On the front steps a young woman is waiting for them. Munteanu approaches her hesitantly, remembering he only ever saw Nora Popescu from a distance in Paralia. *I don't think so. Maybe she looks a bit like Daniel Manole.* Toni follows him closely.

"Hello, gentlemen. I'm Nora Popescu. How may I help you?"

She looks just as refined and elegant as their surroundings: grey skirt, white blouse, a pearl necklace around her neck, discreet make-up, her auburn hair pulled back. Stelian is convinced he's never seen her before.

"Hello, ma'am. My name is Stelian Munteanu and this is my colleague, Toni Demetriade. We were wondering if we could talk to you about the incident in Paralia, if I may call it that? If it's not too much of a bother, of course."

"You don't bother me at all. Please, come in."

The hallway is white with only a few pieces of sculpted furniture, a hallstand and an old chest. The living room is spacious and well lit, with a huge black oak tree; bookcase filled with books, a modern fireplace, dark brown, leather armchairs and sofas, and a giant TV on a stand. In front of the sofas there's a coffee table with an array of bottles, coffee and snacks.

"Please, sit down. Would you like a coffee?"

Nora Popescu doesn't wait for their answer and starts to fill up three porcelain cups. The atmosphere is pleasant and Munteanu starts to relax a little. He remembers the late night coffee over at Eleni's house in Salonica. Nora Popescu smiles easily and innocently, and he's tempted to place her on the innocent characters list. Her skin is pale, she has brown eyes and nails painted discreetly with light pink nail polish. He shakes himself out of his daze and realizes that he has no idea what to ask her.

"Happily. Unfortunately, I know very little about Mircea's activities. And Dan visits us very rarely."

"Mrs. Popescu, you do realize that your sudden departure from Greece only complicated matters further?"

"No doubt. But we believe in Daniel's innocence and my husband thought things would be better off if we returned to Romania while this mess gets sorted out."

"We're not naive, either of us. You do understand that the Greek authorities allowed you to leave. I was in the helicopter following your boat. Your husband believes he can solve everything with his influence. But it's too late. There's an international investigation going on right now and that means the involvement of Interpol."

"I won't comment on any of that."

"Good. Then I'll ask some specific questions."

"I'm listening."

"When did your brother meet the victim?"

"I'm not sure, but I think it was while we were in Paralia. He had never said anything about her until then."

"That means he's not a regular at the Montmartre nightclub?"

"Regular? No! Dan doesn't have a good relationship with Mircea and avoids seeing him at all costs."

"So you're saying your husband is regularly at the Montmartre?"

"Yes. He's good friends with Jacques Colbert, the owner. They are also in business together, although I don't know exactly what kind of business. It never interested me."

"Is Mr. Colbert in Romania right now?"

"As far as I know, no, he is not. But the nightclub has a director and our lawyer represents their interests."

"Can you give us his contact information?"

"Of course. His name is Marcel Dumitru."

She opens a little metal box on the floor next to her and take out a business card. *It's as if she had it ready!*

"There you go. You can call him on his cell phone too. And tell him I gave you his phone number, even though I never give it to anyone."

"Thank you very much, Mrs. Popescu, but we could have found his number by ourselves."

He suddenly realizes that he's being impolite. The tiredness and stress. *I need a serious relationship and a long vacation. Meaning sex, swimming pool and cocktails! And another job, please, while we're at it…*

"I apologize, I didn't mean to offend you. Mister Dumitru was next on our list, especially since he represents your, and Mr. Colbert's, interests. Maybe he knows more about all this."

"Marcel Dumitru was a colleague of mine. Mircea hired him on my recommendation."

"And how did he find Mr. Colbert?"

"I have no idea. I've never met Mr. Colbert."

"Never?"

"No. He only stays in Romania for a few hours. He meets with Mircea and then he leaves."

"Did you know the victim?"

"Only from Dan's stories. I've never been to the Montmartre either. Dan told me about her when we were in Paralia. He was excited, it was passionate. I personally thought it was merely infatuation. The seaside vacation type of love, lasting for no more than a summer…"

"Does Daniel have a girlfriend besides the victim?"

"I don't think so. Maybe he had just separated from someone…I don't remember. You expect me to know too much, gentlemen. My brother doesn't tell me everything."

"Your husband never proposed that they work together?"

"No, I told you they don't have a good relationship. Besides, Dan wants to succeed on his own."

"No offense, Mrs. Popescu, but this sounds like a familiar story." Nora Popescu smiles bitterly.

"Whatever you think about it, it's true. And I don't remember anything about a serious relationship involving my brother and another woman."

"Still, your brother is a suspect."

"There's no proof to support that and no motive for murder. You can't prove Dan used that poison, or that it belonged to him. Plus, he was extremely sincere and cooperated with the authorities."

"You seem to know a lot of details."

"Mircea knows things about it, and the newspapers wrote extensively about it. The death of this girl was unfortunately associated with their affair. And my husband was also implicated."

"Excuse me, but *associated* doesn't quite do justice to their relationship. Even if a motive has not yet been found, your brother is still the number one suspect."

"As you wish, gentleman."

They coolly say their good-byes and the two men leave the villa. Toni starts the engine and backs out slowly. The gate opens.

"You kind of screwed it up at the end, Stelian."

"Rich people games."

"You have to admit, though, that she's okay. Smart and beautiful."

"I wonder why all the smart and beautiful women marry rich, old, ugly men. It's such a cliché."

"Well, you could try it too! You're not too young, not too rich, ugly…so on and so on …"

Munteanu growls.

"You're very funny."

"You didn't say anything about the diamonds. Why?"

"I thought it might be better if I shut up and wait. We're not even certain who knows about it and who doesn't."

"Daniel Manole found out about it in Greece. You really think he didn't tell his sister?"

"I'd prefer to let them act on it."

"I liked the thing with Interpol, though."

"It was a momentary spark of inspiration. She never said anything about the fur coat. She implied that there's no motive for murder. Six big diamonds seem like enough of a motive to me. Toni, let's get serious here. People kill for a lot less than two million euros."

"But you have to admit that Daniel is not the killer. Maybe he's an accomplice, but it's clear there was someone else involved."

"Yeah, we have a long list of possibilities. It makes me dizzy."

"So where to, boss?"

"I'm done. Take me to a cheap, air conditioned restaurant. This car is hell on Earth and I feel like having a good *ciorba*."

"Okay, boss."

"Stop with the *boss* stuff and drive."

It is noon in Salonica. The temperature is well over 40 Celsius. The buildings and streets are boiling, even the tourists are hiding.

Eleni Papastergiu has just returned from the University and is enjoying a long shower. She has no meetings in the city until the evening. She leaves the bathroom, wrapped in a huge pink towel and barefoot, and walks to the kitchen, leaving a wet trail on the cool tiles. She's thirsty and pours herself a big glass of orange juice from a bottle in the fridge. Just in case, she throws in two ice cubes.

She glances at her laptop and notices an unusual new email in her inbox:

> *To Mrs. Eleni Papastergiu,*
> *Salonica University, Mineralogy Department*
>
> *Dear Mrs. Papastergiu,*
>
> *Being aware of the joint Greek and Romanian investigation in Paralia, we are asking for your help in clearing up some aspects regarding the illegal theft happening at the mines in Tarnita. Please accept our urgent invitation to visit us at our*

headquarters in Moscow, from where we will transport you to the site of the mines.

We will pay all the expenses of this trip and offer you an allowance in accordance with the international standards. The trip will only take three days of your time.

We hope to receive a positive answer as soon as possible to plan all the details.

Sincerely,

Director,
Dr. ing. Valeri Ripkin

Eleni studies the heading: *The Russian Federation. National Agency for Protection and Development of Natural Resources.* Then the address, phone number, fax and email address. She hasn't heard of this particular agency, but, because of all the reforms in the ex-communist countries, the state departments regularly change their names and addresses. She checks her schedule and finds that she can go, even for a week, with no major problems. She can cancel her classes and then work harder to catch up. She really is excited for a bit of a summer adventure. *At least it should be cooler in Moscow.* She quickly answers the email.

TEN

THE SUN IS SETTING, TINTING THE PASSING CLOUDS IN SHADES of red. A beautiful sunset in dusty Bucharest. The Montmartre nightclub is an ugly, square and huge building. It probably was once an old sports complex. A big multicoloured sign brightly flashes in garish bad taste. At the entrance a bodyguard asks members for their IDs, but tonight police IDs seem to be enough.

Ionel Pavel, the director, is waiting for them. A small, round, man, he's bald, with a red face and thick lips. He stands in a room that is cramped and windowless.

"Good evening. I was waiting for you."

"Good evening, Mr. Pavel."

"Sit down, gentlemen. No need to introduce yourselves. I know who you are. What would you like me to show or tell you?"

"I'll be brief. When did you last see Mr. Jacques Colbert?"

The small, bald man sighs. He's not arrogant, he seems tired and a bit overwhelmed by the events. He looks like a accountant or restaurant maitre d'.

"I've never seen Mr. Colbert!"

This was a complete surprise.

"What do you mean *never*?"

"These were the conditions: He only meets with his lawyer, Marcel Dumitru, and business associate, Mircea Popescu. I receive written instructions, or the lawyer informs me of whatever Mr. Colbert wants me to do."

"And this doesn't seem a bit strange to you?"

"I have a decent salary and I learned long ago not to ask questions. Plus, I don't break the law. They've never asked me to do anything illegal."

"We weren't implying that. It just seems a bit weird to me, that's all."

"There are a lot of weird things in our country."

"Do you have a lot of customers?" Munteanu changes the subject.

"In the summer, especially out on the terrace. The girls have to take turns with their vacations."

"Any foreign girls?"

"We have eight girls in total, they dance in pairs, sometimes four of them in one evening, depending on the requests. All of them are from the former Soviet Union."

"No Romanians?"

"No. They're more expensive. And this was the owner's wish."

"Meaning?"

"He asked me not to hire Romanian girls."

"Why is that?"

"I don't know. Maybe he didn't want any problems with the families. I didn't ask."

"Interesting. Do you know if Mr. Colbert has businesses in Russia?

"I really can't say. I have no idea and I'm not interested in knowing."

"When do you expect Galia Kalughina to come back to work?"

"She still has a few more vacation days. She'll be back on Monday. But she told me she'll come by tonight, so you can talk to her if you want."

"Do you know what time she's coming?"

"She should be here any minute."

"Why did you send a car to pick her up?"

"She called me. She was scared. Dumitru was here and he made the decision. I did what I was told. I would have done it anyway, regardless. She's our employee, it's normal to help her. Her boyfriend, Doru, who's also a bodyguard here, drove to the Golden Sands to pick her up. She was waiting for him at a hotel."

"Doru?"

"Doru Stan. He's a law student and works for us."

"Romanian?"

"Yes. Except for the girls, all of our staff is Romanian."

"What about all of the trips to France?"

"Mr. Colbert arranged auditions for the girls. Two of them obtained contracts and are dancing over there now. Only Tania went two or three times, God rest her soul. Short stints. I don't know why she didn't stay longer. She never told me and I never asked. Galia was next, then another girl, Milena."

"Is Milena here?"

"No, she's in Estonia visiting her parents."

"When was she supposed to leave?"

"At the beginning of the month. But it seems that things have been moved up for Galia. I received an email from the owner today. She might leave in a day or two for a couple of days. She'll be back on Monday."

"What do you mean she might?"

"Well, the boss told me to get her ready. He's sending her the flight tickets."

"Okay, thanks for your help. We'll be waiting out on the terrace."

"Of course. Would you like something to drink?"

"No, thank you."

"A non-alcoholic beer?"

"Yes, that would be fine. Thanks."

They sit at a round table with two chairs and a red umbrella. The waiter appears right away with the cold beers, glasses and an ashtray. Only a few other tables are taken, so they're mostly alone.

"He seems kind of desperate to stick to *no* and *I don't know*, don't you think?"

"The man wants to retire in peace. He knows to keep quiet."

"The circle is closing."

"Yeah. If it didn't go well with Tania maybe they'll be more successful with Galia."

"Are you going to arrest her?"

"I should, but we have no proof."

"So what do we do?"

"I'll wait here. You should go to the office. Contact someone in France and tell them to find this Jacques Colbert. Find that lawyer too. We can't wait until tomorrow. And find out where Popescu is now. I'll take care of Galia. But after, put her under observation, just in case. We need more people from your boss. Think you can convince him?"

"I'll take care of it."

"Whatever time it is, if there's news you let me know. I'll have my phone with me at all times. Otherwise, pick me up tomorrow at eight."

"Eight?"

"Yes. We'll be running around a lot. It'll be a long day so make sure you get some rest."

"Okay. You want me to leave you the car?"

"No, I'll take a taxi. Good night, Toni."

"Good night."

"One more thing, Toni."

"Yes."

"Get your boss to give us another car. Please ..."

"I'll get on it"

He disappears toward the parking lot.

Jacques Sardi is enjoying a pastry. Only the regular customers are relaxing at La Belle Parisienne, his favourite café. He has no more snobbish parties to attend tonight, no more superficial polite conversations with rich women showing off their diamonds. The first horse racing announcements appear on the TV screen when his phone starts ringing. *Merde. I wanted to watch this. Again I won't know the results.*

Everyone around is annoyed, so he has to answer.

"Oui."

"Sardi, something's come up," the voice at the other end sounds nervous and stressed. "Some weird affair with diamonds and a murder in Greece. A Russian-Romanian cartel. Forget the ladies and get your ass over here."

"I was having a peaceful drink. No ladies."

"Well, drink up, you and get here now! We're talking six diamonds the size of walnuts."

"Merde! I'm on my way."

He finishes his drink, says his good-byes and rushes off to his car. This case might have promise ... six diamonds like walnuts. Interesting. But the late hour is a real pain. *You don't start work at eleven o'clock at night!*

"So, we meet again, Mr. Munteanu."

Galia watches him with a wry smile, standing next to the table.

"Good evening. You remember my name."

"Not really. I had to ask my boss."

"I see you speak Romanian very well."

"I wanted to learn it and my boyfriend helped me."

"Sit down."

"I actually wanted to suggest something else. I'm all done here, so I thought maybe we could go to my place. We can talk in peace without any interference."

Stelian hesitates, but the proposition is tempting. The loud music bugs him. And Galia is smiling invitingly.

"Don't worry, Mr. Policeman, I won't bite."

"You might not like the direction of our conversation. Maybe a neutral spot is more appropriate."

"Let's cut the crap, Mr. Munteanu. My vacation was ruined too. Besides, a private discussion before I'm called into the police station can only help both of us."

"It's not too professional."

"You're not really a policeman, though, so I think you can make an exception."

"Alright then, let's go."

Stelian stands and they exit together. Galia drives a red Dacia Logan. She gets behind the wheel and starts the engine with confidence. Stelian starts to think that maybe this was a bad idea. Her discreet perfume tickles his nose. Maybe Chanel Chance? She's dressed elegantly, in dark blue trousers and a white blouse. She doesn't look at all like the party girl he'd seen in Paralia. She drives the car onto Ştefan cel Mare Boulevard and continues on Mihai Bravu. The city is still buzzing, but the traffic has died down. Stelian feels sleepy and he misses Paralia. He starts to daydream about the Greek woman's face in her apartment in Salonica and goes into a slumber...

"We're here."

They are on the Călăraşi Boulevard, close to the Hurmuzachi Market, or Vergului, or Muncii, whatever the hell it's called now. Galia parks the car on the street, and they exit and walk to her building.

"I have a small two-room apartment," she answers his silent question.

"Rented?"

"No, I bought it."

"So I gather you make good money? An apartment here is quite expensive."

"I got a good price for it."

"And you paid for it in cash?"

"No, credit."

She unlocks the door and invites him inside.

The living room is decorated tastefully, without extravagance. A couch, two armchairs, a coffee table with bottles and glasses, a phone, a bookshelf, a nice lamp. Nothing unusually expensive. On the walls there are two ink drawings and a photo of Galia at a fashion show. There are two porcelain figurines on the bookshelf and a bronze candleholder with two arms surrounded by a few framed photos. In a corner, there's a diploma written in Russian.

Stelian carefully scans the room, but can't find anything suspicious; there's nothing out of place. Even the stereo sound system doesn't look too new or expensive. He starts to wonder if he hasn't formed the wrong impression about the party girl he met in Paralia. First impressions can be so wrong sometimes. He pours himself a bit of Metaxa and feels like having a cigarette, but opts against it. A pack of Dunhills on one of the shelves catches his eye and Misha Pushkin's pops into his head. She smokes the same cigarettes as the KGB man.

When Galia returns to the room he realizes that he hadn't known she was gone. Galia has changed into a dark red, silk robe showing a generous amount of cleavage, and his heart starts racing as he absently pulls at his tie. She's wearing nothing underneath. She turns off the lamp, leaving only a small orange night-light. Quietly she pours herself a shot of vodka from an open bottle. *She lights a cigarette with a golden lighter. Smirnoff and Dunhill.*

Munteanu devours her with his eyes and sips his cognac. He chokes and the glass trembles in his hand. He notices her perfect body, her tanned, smooth skin. His eyes caress her whole body. He blushes when he realizes what he's doing. Still, his eyes are drawn to her cleavage. Her breasts are attracting him like two big flutes of champagne, making him dizzy.

"May I call you by your first name?"

Her words echo in his ears. She smiles and approaches him, touches her glass to his. And keeps it there.

"Cheers."

Munteanu experiences a quick flash of memories. High school, college, his failed marriage… *How stupid!* Galia's perfume seduces him completely. The silk robe rustles enticingly and slips away slowly, revealing her body little by little. They watch each other with barely restrained need. She's closer and closer and Munteanu asks himself why he should resist her? Except for the fact that she's could be an accomplice in an international murder and diamond smuggling case. Ah, b*ut what the hell, we're only human!* Their lips are touching and he feels a fresh aroma. Cold and warm. Hot. His hand touches her. The robe slips off a little more…

"I got you!"

They both jump, like waking from a bad dream. Drops of cognac and vodka spill on the couch and their clothing. A tall man, dressed in black overalls decorated with dozens of badges, looms over them. He's holding a bat in one hand and pepper spray in the other.

"That's why you left so quickly from the nightclub?! To impress the police?"

Munteanu drifted from a dream to a living a nightmare. A few seconds ago he was kissing a gorgeous woman and now he's being threatened by a furious giant.

"Get dressed. I'll teach him a lesson he won't forget."

"Doru, calm down! This is really stupid!"

Munteanu starts to understand. The situation doesn't look good at all. The angry man steps forward. This is becoming dangerous. Galia stands and tries to interfere. Doru pushes her into an armchair. Stelian thinks frantically to find a solution. He shifts on the couch and something nudges him on his left side. He smiles suddenly and puts his hand underneath his jacket. There's a metallic click and the bodyguard takes another step to find the Beretta glued to his chest. He looks down at the barrel and drops the bat and pepper spray. His eyes are as big as saucers as he steps back.

"I would love to tell you *freeze* like in the American movies!"

The bodyguard doesn't seem to hear him and keeps stepping backwards. Munteanu takes aim, holding the gun with both hands, wondering if he might actually need to use the gun to stop him.

"Hey, take it easy. You heard the man, freeze. Don't make this harder than it already is."

Toni is standing at the threshold of the open door, pointing an identical gun.

"Calvary is here?"

"You better believe it!"

Doru collapses in a chair. Five more men storm into the room, three of them dressed in police uniforms. Metal handcuffs come out.

"Take'em in, guys. Both of them. Boss, I've got a surprise for you."

Stelian starts to calm down and returns his gun to its holster. *Never thought I would need this thing.* That's when he notices that one of the men in the doorway is Iannis Theodopoulos.

ELEVEN

ALTHOUGH THE SKY STARTS TO LIGHTEN COME MORNING, lights still burn in many of the offices of the General Inspectorate building. The streets are quiet and deserted. The billboards are dark and the city looks grey. Traffic lights obsessively blink yellow. Only a few early morning pedestrians hurry on the sidewalks.

On the third floor, the briefing room is brightly lit and looks like a battlefield: plastic glasses, sandwiches, note books, pens, laptops, a few sketches, two maps and six men. The men not in uniform are Munteanu, Demetriade and Theodopoulos. The other three are dressed in Romanian Police uniforms. Stelian rubs his face with his hands and wishes that he could pour a glass of mineral water into his head.

"Anyone else want more coffee?" one of the policemen asks.

Nobody answers.

"Go home and get some sleep, Toni. I'll stay with Iannis. There's another long day ahead of us and it would be good if one of us had a clear head."

Toni doesn't comment, but when he walks to the exit the door opens and the chief enters. Chief Inspector Asaftei deftly hides his displeasure with being dragged in so early. It didn't help that he just left an argument with his wife over his, more or less, strict parenting methods.

"Good morning, gentlemen. What's the news?"

He turns toward Theodopoulos and addresses him in English.

"Welcome to Romania."

Iannis mumbles his thanks. He looks as dizzy as Munteanu.

"I won't keep you from your work. I only wanted to let you know that you can count on my assistance. Stelian, check your computer, you might have new information in regards to Mr. Colbert. Inspector Sardi from the Parisian police department dealing with stolen art and jewelry took over our case. I wish you good luck. I'll be in my office if you need me."

With that, he exits. Nobody says anything. Toni mutters his goodbyes and exits as well. The others start to clean up. In a corner, Stelian and Iannis sit on two old brown armchairs that look as if they're remnants of the old regime.

"All these new characters are confusing me, Stelios."

"You mean the bodyguard?"

"Not just him. He might simply be a jealous boyfriend. And Galia is the type of woman you could attack a policeman for."

"I wonder."

"Even if he's implicated, he's not the key to the puzzle. There's another brain behind all this."

"Popescu and his clique over at the Montmartre, starting with the elusive Colbert. Even Nora Popescu didn't seem sincere to me either."

"The lawyer is the key. Has anyone seen him? Does he even exist?"

"Allegedly he does, we have his biography, diplomas, pictures. He's accompanying Popescu to Chişinău."

"Honestly, I think the Popescu-Colbert-Dumitru triangle is hiding a big mystery. You're telling me that Colbert doesn't meet with his nightclub manager, only with this lawyer and Popescu?"

"It happens. Maybe he's a busy."

"No, it doesn't make any sense."

"What are you saying?"

"I don't think the lawyer even exists."

"I don't understand, we have a lot of data on him."

"It could all be fabricated. I think the lawyer is really Colbert."

"That's impossible, Iannis! Marcel Dumitru is Romanian. You can't mistake a Romanian for a Frenchman."

"Then maybe it's the other way around. Nobody's ever seen this Colbert."

"I don't see the motivation. Besides, it's the same thing; you can't convince anyone that a Romanian can play a Frenchman convincingly. And I'm not only talking about the language barrier..."

"The motivation? What about a foreign cover story in case he has problems in Romania. Properties and wealth in France for when he retires. Not to mention that his diamond friends are French, and being a Frenchman inspires more trust."

"Maybe. Romanians don't have such a good reputation for business."

"I didn't mean that, Stelios."

"You didn't have to. We all know it."

Stelian stands and walks to an open laptop.

"Maybe now we'll know more."

He finds an email with multiple attachments from the French Police. He downloads everything and waves over Iannis to join him. The others have just finished cleaning the room.

"Thank you. I'll let you know when we reach a conclusion."

They are left alone. Outside, the sky starts to turn purple. Cars and pedestrians start to invade the streets. Stelian opens a file labelled *colbert.doc*. The document pops up on the screen.

There's an old, fogged picture of a hippy wearing glasses, with a date of birth.

"Impossible! Date of birth 21 of March 1951?! There's no way!"

"So your theory fails, Iannis. Dumitru is barely forty. He was in college with Nora Popescu, remember?"

"So it's back to the old what came first, the chicken or the egg? In our case, the Romanian or the Frenchman?"

"I think we're losing ourselves in details. We're better off finding any of them. We're missing something."

On the screen there's a series of biographical details: born in Rouen, Normandy, elementary and high school in Rouen, accountant at the Jean Rance & Cie, promoted as a Development Director, an apartment in the 14th Arondissement of Paris, another in Marseille, import-export firm doing business in Africa and Eastern Europe.

"Look at this, Stelios. In 1990 he came to Romania to establish a few commercial firms and financed scholarships for Romanian students in France."

"But we're missing their names."

"We've got the company he used as a sponsor. We can contact the participating schools."

"Why do I feel like we're complicating everything?"

"You're right, I'll stop. Let's sum it all up. We have a young Frenchman coming to Romania. He's a wealthy business man, maybe trying to get access to state finances and covers it all up with scholarships. He meets Nora Popescu and finds out her husband has businesses in Russia. They meet and become associates, then open the nightclub as a front for illegal diamond smuggling."

"There are big gaps in your theory, Iannis. How does the Frenchman suddenly become a younger Romanian? And Nora wasn't Popescu's wife at that time."

"True. But still, my intuition tells me that Colbert is someone else."

"I want to know who was waiting for the girls when they arrived in France."

"Which girls?"

"The dancers transporting the fur coats."

"Probably Colbert, or someone working for him."

"So there is a chance that Galia knows him. If she's been to Paris that means she could have met him. Maybe she'll open up a little after spending a night in jail."

"I've got another question. Where are Popescu and the lawyer right now? Are they back in the country yet?"

Stelian freezes for a second, then picks up the phone and asks to be transferred to the border police.

"This is Munteanu, Mr. Chief Inspector. We're still looking for Mircea Popescu and Marcel Dumitru. Can you tell me where they are? Are they back?"

"Just a second, I'll check."

There's silence, then the voice over the speaker.

"This is very weird, Mr. Munteanu, but I'll tell you nonetheless. After embarking in Otopeni on a Tarom flight to Chișinău, they changed their mind and left the flight during a stopover in Iasi."

"So they never left the country?"

"Apparently not. It's strange to change your mind during the flight, especially you've already passed border inspection at the airport."

"And they didn't continue their trip by car or train?"

"No. They don't appear anywhere at the Moldavian border. They remained in the country. But... wait a minute. Marcel Dumitru's name popped up today."

"Today? Where?"

"At the Turnu border, just past midnight."

"Alone?"

"I don't know. We had orders to monitor him, not detain him. I don't have any more information. Is it serious?"

"Very."

"I'll try to get more information and I'll let you know as soon as I hear something."

"Thank you and please hurry!"

"I will do everything I can. But you must understand we can't detain or question people leaving the country without a written warrant. Goodbye."

Stelian slams the phone down.

"We've got a big problem, Iannis. The race is still on. Our lawyer fled the country in the middle of the night! He could be all the way to Austria by now."

Misha Pushkin is guides his old metal razor with the skill and finesse of a Bolshoi dancer. On the bathroom shelf next to him there's a cup of Earl Grey tea and a smoking Dunhill in an ashtray. He's finished. He surveys his work in the mirror and pours some Old Spice cologne into his palm to rub it on his face. That done, he returns to the spacious, white furnished room with the cigarette in his hand. The Anna Hotel is quite expensive, but then all hotels are expensive in Vienna. At least this one is discreet and very central. If nothing unexpected comes up, he can take a walk through the famous Prater park. He can ride the giant Ferris wheel, shoot a few targets to win a toy bear, then have a schnitzel and a good coffee in a little bistro.

He picks a grey shirt and a pair of trousers from his closet, then adjusts the Glock under his armpit. He covers the gun with a light jacket, collects his keys, cigarettes and a lighter, and then locks the door. He needs a good breakfast. The young receptionist smiles at him like a programmed robot.

"Mr. Pushkin?"

"That's me."

"You have a message."

Pushkin takes the paper. *They preferred not to call. Old habits die hard. It's more secure anyways.* He sits down in one of the armchairs. On the paper there are two sentences in Russian:

The coat is in Pressbaum, first exit on the A1 toward Salzburg. Parzer Bed & Breakfast in the city centre, 100 m to the left.

We'll take care of the Greek woman this morning.

He folds the paper and puts it in his pocket. *I'll destroy it later. Seems like I'll have to eat my breakfast over in Pressbaum. So much for a stroll in Vienna...*

A Russian Aeroflot Tupolev 154 lands at Seremetievo Airport. The old plane is only half full. Eleni stuffs the two magazines she bought before leaving in her hand luggage. The flight was easy, no problems. She ate and slept for an hour or so. She's full of energy. A bus is waiting for the passengers at the exit. She grabs her luggage and gets her passport ready for inspection. The section reserved for EU citizens is almost empty. Maybe after finishing with her work she could visit a few museums. Ever since the mines were closed five or six years ago, she hadn't been invited to Russia.

"Mrs. Eleni Papastergiu, coming from Salonica?" someone asks in English.

She turns to see two men dressed in dark suits. They both attempt to smile, but their faces are as cold as ice.

"Yes, that's me."

"Please, follow us."

"Is something wrong?"

"We can't discuss it later. Please, follow us."

"Where to?"

"Don't worry, we'll explain everything at the airport's command centre."

She follows them without comment. Her Russian adventure has started faster than she expected.

Two cars park in front of the Popescu residence. A SWAT team of masked men silently descend from the VW Transporter Syncro. Two policemen dressed in different uniforms exit from the other car, a VW Passat. The chief inspector, Asaftei, and Iannis. In a few minutes Toni's old Dacia arrives at the scene, with Munteanu alongside. The SWAT team fans out around the perimeter while the others stand in front of the metal gate as it quickly opens.

In front of the house there are three scared looking people: a man and two women. None of them are who they're looking for.

"I'm chief inspector Asaftei. We have a search warrant."

One of the middle aged women answers:

"I am the maid. Mr. and Mrs. Popescu are not home."

"When did they leave?"

Stelian hides a yawn. He predicted all of this. The border agents had informed him that Dumitru was not alone in the car. He was accompanied by a woman.

"Mr. Popescu is in Chișinău and Mrs. Popescu left last night with her lawyer."

"Did she say where she was going?"

"No. She asked me to pack a suitcase for a few days. She said it's something urgent and that she'll call in the afternoon."

"Was she wearing a fur coat?" Munteanu interferes. "Or did she pack one in the suitcase?"

"A fur coat in the summer? No."

"Thank you. Well now we know. Let's take off now, we're not going to find anything here."

Asaftei watches him with puzzled eyes. So does Iannis, who doesn't understand a word of the conversation.

"Alright. The three of you can give written statements to the officers," the chief inspector orders, then turns toward Stelian.

"If all of this is so obvious to you, why don't you explain it to us?"

"The fur coat never made it to Romania, sir. They left it in Rome during the stopover."

"Wrong. Why did they return to Romania then? They could have gone straight to Paris."

Toni translates for Iannis.

"Stelios, the fur coat was here. Everything had to look right. The girls had to have clothes in their suitcases while traveling to France."

"The hell it looked right, Iannis. Who needs a fur coat in Paris in the summer?"

They switch to English and Toni jumps in:

"Gentlemen, Galia has the answers to our questions. Like Stelian said, she'll probably cooperate now after spending a night in jail. I suggest we return to the headquarters and pry it out of her."

Asaftei nods.

"Good idea. Take the two gentlemen with you. I'll stay to make sure we search every corner of this house."

Munteanu smiles bitterly at Iannis.

"How about some coffee, Iannis?"

The Greek detective responds with his own look of dejection.

"Where did your colleague go?"

They realize they're standing alone in the garden.

Pushkin has parked by a supermarket right across the street from the bed and breakfast. He's a bit exposed. There's only a few cars around and he's worried that the dark blue Range Rover Vogue will attract unwanted attention. He puts his hand on his gun and surveys the windows across the street. The ground floor is surely not used for tourists. Behind the flower pots he can't see any pulled curtains. Two windows are open at the first floor. In the parking lot there are only three cars: an old Ford Transit, a yellow VW Polo and a black BMW 5. He bets the BMW has Romanian plates. There's a shadow moving behind one of the open windows. His heart starts to beat faster. The enemy could have binoculars and might have recognized him. He starts the engine and drives out of the parking lot onto the main street. There has be a coffee shop open somewhere. The Austrian Police will arrive in about twenty minutes with orders to detain the two Romanians. He has enough time for an espresso and a cigarette.

Nora Popescu is in a daze. Marcel sped like mad to get them here. A hot shower sounds heavenly. As she enjoys the warmth of the water on her skin, she mulls over the past few days. The police coming to her house. Marcel's nervousness, his endless, repulsive flirting, Mircea's message urgently calling them to Paris, weirdly enough by car and not by plane; a sign that something was wrong. Maybe Mircea and Marcel have hatched some plan, perhaps even Daniel, who has vanished. She feels dizzy and leans against the tiled wall, touching the cold water tap by mistake. The shock snaps her back to reality.

Stelian and Iannis are puzzled. Where did Toni disappear to? But their confusion only lasts a few seconds. A white VW Passat breaks hard right next to them and there he is, with the look of a NYPD cop:

"Get in! Time is short. Galia is waiting for us at headquarters, then we're off again. They've found Nora and the lawyer at a bed and breakfast twelve kilometers west of Vienna, right off the A1 highway. The Austrian Police are certain they have the right people!"

They get in without comment. Stelian feels like he's walking into a Jules Verne novel. *If I keep it up, I'll be around the world in eighty days… Bucharest, Paralia, Skiathos, Rome, Bucharest and now Vienna. I should keep a journal. Maybe I can make some money…* He feels his gun again, and again wonders if he will be forced to use it. He remembers Galia's silk robe slipping away and what was underneath. Then the white marble image of the Greek woman in Salonica replaces the Russian woman's face. *Where is she now? I should look her up. Maybe get her phone number from…*

Marcel Dumitru feels an emptiness in his stomach. It's due to hunger, not worry. He has managed to sneak out of the country without any problems. Only a thousand-or-so kilometers and they'll be in Paris. Still, he feels a touch of anxiety. *Are they really that stupid, or are they just waiting?* He silently opens the bathroom door. Nora is still in the shower. There's no reason for her to hurry and she's probably still in shock. Everything will settle soon. Soon he'll be on a flight to French Guiana from Paris and then Brazil, Venezuela, maybe even the Caribbean Islands. They'll never find him.

What about Mircea? Will Nora run away with him, or stick with her husband? After all, we're lawyers! A ménage à trois? Stupid! Ridiculous! He admires himself in the mirror: well-trained, tanned, athletic body. Well-defined face, freshly shaved, black hair, blue eyes. *I'm still young, and there are many lonely women out there.* He glances out the window. The fur coat is in his suitcase in the trunk of the car. The car looks fine. Of course it is, they're in Austria.

His eyes scan the supermarket parking lot. Only a few cars. A white Opel Zafira drives by slowly, going around the building. *That's strange, that's a lot of people inside that car. Who goes out shopping at this hour with the whole family?* He's suspicious. He grabs the room key and leaves, locks the door from the outside, and slips a Smith & Wesson 36 in his jacket. *Just in case...*

In the command centre of the Seremetievo Airport, there are a few men dressed in dark suits and Eleni Papastergiu. She is seated in a comfortable armchair in front of a small table containing an array of papers and black and white pictures.

"Mrs. Papastergiu, let me repeat what I said, you've been set up. *The National Agency for the Protection and Development of Natural Resources* does not exist. The address listed here is an apartment building. And we don't know a Valeri Ripkin."

"This is unbelievable! What did they want from me?"

"With all due respect, what they wanted was you...gone."

"To kill me? But why?"

"Maybe not kill you, jut eliminate you as a problem. You're too close. You've seen the mines, you know the stones, and now they know the Greek Police brought you in as an expert."

"Sorry, but who are the *they* you're speaking of?"

"Well, them and us more like it."

"Them? Please be more specific!"

"If we knew who they were it would be a lot simpler. This whole thing is international. And we have to be careful about Russia's image. We can't make any official statements. For now. Besides, there's a flight to Vienna waiting for you. Mr. Theodopoulos from the Greek Police is waiting for you there, with the Romanian and Austrian authorities. Perhaps Vienna is better than Moscow for a short vacation."

Eleni is overwhelmed. This is a lot to take in.

"So what do I have to do?"

"We'll escort you to the departure gate. Your flight to Vienna leaves in half an hour."

"What about the diamonds? And the mines in Tarnita?"

"I'm afraid I can't give you an answer to that. It's not the police's problem. The Ministry will take care of it and the government will decide something once this investigation is over. But let's not get ahead of ourselves. Follow us, please."

Without explanation, she is escorted to the her gate. Two plain-clothed officers carry her luggage. She shrugs with resignation. *I don't have a choice! Vienna could be better than Moscow. I've never been to Vienna...*

TWELVE

GALIA SITS IN THE POLICE INTERROGATION ROOM, WHICH seems huge in the sunlight. After a night in jail, any confidence she had is shot. Her face is free of make-up and she has dark shadows around her eyes. Toni Demetriade signals the two agents guarding her to leave. He takes a seat, followed by Munteanu and Theodopoulos.

"We'll talk in Romanian. Toni, please translate for Iannis."

Munteanu turns to Galia. He keeps his eyes on her as he pours a glass of water and sips it.

"Would you like some water?"

"No."

The tension is palpable.

"Galia, we're out of time. Your situation has taken a turn for the worse, so do yourself a favour and give us some answers. OK?"

"OK."

"How did you end up in Bulgaria?"

"I don't know. When I woke up, a man talked to me in Russian and introduced himself as the Russian cultural attaché in Sofia. He told me my life was in danger and asked me to call Bucharest for a ride home."

"He didn't say anything else?"

"No. I was scared. He told me someone was going to try to kidnap me and that he saved me at the last moment. I called the Montmartre and talked to my manager, then to Doru. He came over by car."

"But how did you get to Bulgaria?"

"I don't remember. Honestly! I remember going to a party and then waking up in a hotel room in Zlatni Piasaci."

"The man you are talking about, was he about sixty?"

"Yes, and he smoked Dunhills. I remember that because Tania smoked the same brand with the big red package."

Munteanu and Theodopoulos exchange a look. Pushkin!

"But I remember seeing the same kind of cigarettes in your apartment. You even smoked a cigarette from it."

"They were Tania's. I brought them from Greece as a kind of reminder of her. I rarely smoke."

"You shouldn't smoke at all. We will search your apartment and check the pack of cigarettes. Maybe we'll find other fingerprints."

"No comment."

"When were you supposed to leave for Paris?"

"In two, maybe three, days. I was waiting for my ticket."

"Who reserved your flight?"

"The club manager, Mr. Pavel."

"Have you ever seen the French owner?"

"No. Never."

"The name Colbert sound familiar?"

"No."

"Do you even know the French owner's name?"

"We were all hired by Mr. Pavel."

"What about Marcel Dumitru?"

"Yes, I know him. He's the lawyer of the firm. He's around thirty-something and a snob. Expensive sunglasses and clothes, spray tanned, drives a fancy car. I don't like him, he's full of himself."

"Mircea Popescu?"

"Someone pointed him out one day. He knew Mr. Pavel and the lawyer, but never interacted with us. I don't know much about him. I heard rumours that he's rich and involved in politics. But, like I said, I only saw him at the nightclub once."

"Did you know he was in Paralia too?"

"No, I didn't."

"Was he more acquainted with any of the other girls?"

"I don't know. I told you, I've never seen him talking to any of us."

"What about Tania's boyfriend, Daniel Manole. Do you know him?"

"Who's Daniel Manole?"

"The one suspected of her murder."

"The guy from Greece? I met him there. Tania introduced him one evening, but she kept him away from me. She was afraid I would steal him."

"Was their relationship serious?"

"God knows. Tania was full of secrets. She was supposed to leave for France and she wanted to take him with her."

"When did they propose for you to go to France?"

"When I got back here."

"Why now?"

"I was replacing Tania. She had a contract and I had to go to an audition in her place."

"Who was going to meet you over there?"

"I don't know. Someone was going to pick me up from the airport."

"Did you know that Mircea Popescu and Daniel Manole were relatives?"

"What kind of relatives?"

"Mr. Popescu's wife is Daniel's sister. They're brothers-in-law."

"I didn't know that. I've never heard anything about Mrs. Popescu."

"What about the other girls who went to France?"

"There were only two others. I've never met them, but I've heard about them. They never came back. They got contracts and stayed."

"Is that what you wanted as well?"

"Isn't that what we all want? A better salary? I don't see anything wrong with that!"

" Are you aware of the clothes they took with them?"

"I don't understand."

"The clothing they packed for France."

"How am I supposed to know that?"

"Well, then what kind of clothing were you planning to pack?"

"Again, I don't understand your question."

"Did anyone suggest anything in particular? Maybe the club manager?"

"No, but I knew what was required. Two or three formal outfits, one very sexy, one elegant."

"Nothing to stay warm?"

"What exactly do you mean by *warm*?"

"A fur coat goddammit!" Munteanu explodes.

"Fur coat?! You're obsessed with fur coats, aren't you? Why would I need a fur coat in the summer?"

"OK, fine. We're done, thank you."

He calls in one of the agents to escort her out. *I don't think I've ever heard so many evasive answers in my whole life!*

"She's playing us."

"I don't think so. She's too scared. Popescu is the one playing us. He's causing us to lose precious time, Stelios. Let's get to Vienna, this girl doesn't know anything else."

Marcel Dumitru sits at a restaurant table. He has ordered a schnitzel with French fries and a beer. He's the only one in the place. The tables are set, awaiting customers: nice napkins, shiny plates, stainless steel dining service, with menus at each table.

At the bar, the young owner Jürgen Parzer wipes glasses with a blue kitchen towel and absently watches a football game on TV. Now and then he inspects his work in the light. He doesn't pay any attention to Marcel. Like in an American movie.

Marcel was very thirsty. The frosted beer mug in front of him is already half empty. It's cold and good. With a feeling of unease, he grabs his gun and slides it under a napkin. The owner doesn't notice; he's wrapped up in his football game. It's a rerun, but he doesn't know the score and watches it like it's live.

The door opens and a man enters. He's dressed in a grey suit, blue shirt and no tie. He nods at the owner and stands at the bar. They talk quietly. The owner stops wiping his glasses and frowns. He's worried. Petrified. Dumitru feels the room close in on him. He looks out the window, it's quiet. Parzer throws him a scared look. The man at the bar turns, reaches inside his jacket and opens his mouth to say something. That's when the first bullet shatters the quiet, hitting the man in the shoulder. The second one whizzes past the owner and shatters some glasses. The wounded man crashes to the floor. The owner remains pinned to the wall. Dumitru slowly stands and heads for the exit…

Almost simultaneously, the restaurant's windows explode, as bullets thud into the tables and walls. Dumitru remains standing, and returns fire. The wounded man reaches for his gun, but another bullet stops him. A new salvo of bullets snap from the darkness outside.

The Dumitru continues to return fire, but a new, deafening blast, shot from somewhere closer by, takes him down. A high calibre lethal shot.

***

Nora Popescu walks out of the bathroom, wrapped in a white towel. She's applying perfume when she hears the first shots. She jumps and looks out the window, but can't see any police cars in front of the hotel. She hears more gunfire, followed by a deafening blast.

She faints before she can hear the calm after the storm.

The restaurant is a mess of glass and debris. Steiner, the Austrian inspector, wounded in his shoulder and hip, is placed on a stretcher, but he refuses to be taken to the waiting ambulance. First aid is applied right there. Misha Pushkin steps out from behind a wooden stairwell and places his Glock 20 back in its holster. He lights a cigarette and identifies himself. Parzer the owner is shaken but unharmed. He pours coffee in a few cups. A mix of Police, still holding their weapons, civilians and medical personnel fill up the restaurant.

Marcel Dumitru is dead, with a 10ᵐᵐ bullet lodged in his heart. The cameras and plastic bags have been brought out. Evidence is collected and examined.

"Herr Pushkin, it would have been better if your aim wasn't so precise. He only had one bullet left in his gun," Steiner barks from the stretcher.

"True, but that bullet could have killed someone. Maybe even you. The third shot could have been lethal. Besides, I didn't have time to count. Everything happened so fast."

"You need to give a full statement. We have strong restrictions on people carrying guns in Austria."

"You can rest assured that your Ministry of Internal Affairs knows everything. I was the one to tip you off about the arrival of the two suspects in Pressbaum in the first place."

Pushkin crushes his cigarette in an ashtray.

"Now, please excuse me. My job isn't done. I wish you a speedy recovery, inspector."

He makes a theatrical exit. Nobody stops him.

THIRTEEN

IT TAKES A FEW HOURS IN THE SMALL PLANE TO FLY FROM Băneasa, to Vienna. Then, they drive with flashing lights and sirens through the busy Austrian capital to finally arrive in Pressbaum.

The normally peaceful small town is unusually a hive of activity. Next to the police surrounding the scene there's the growing crowd of press. Cars are parked in front of the bar and two local television vans are broadcasting live. The Austrian police guard the entrance, but the Romanian delegation is allowed through.

The restaurant looks better now. The glass and debris has been cleaned up. With the help of his wife, owner Jürgen Parzer has relaxed enough to play host to the growing crowd. Inspector Steiner manages to shake the newcomers' hands despite his wounds, which are not as bad as initially thought. He's more bothered with the bandages. They chat in English, while Parzer hands out sandwiches, coffee and beer.

Nore Popescu, the only woman in the room, is crying silently in a corner. Seated in a chair and covered with a blanket, she has recovered enough from fainting to learn that Dumitru was in a shootout with the police and had been killed. She's in total shock and they have given her a sedative to calm down.

"Gentlemen, the information we received proved to be correct. Apparently this Herr Pushkin knew what was going on. Unfortunately, Marcel Dumitru was killed during the confrontation. Even though he saved my life, amd probably also saved the restaurant owner's life, I still think Pushkin should have had better aim. Who knows, maybe it was a mistake..."

"Pushkin doesn't make mistakes, inspector," Munteanu interferes nervously. "He's always a step ahead."

Visibly disturbed, the Austrian inspector continues:

"I'll take your word on that. The problem is we can't interrogate our suspect anymore. Mrs. Popescu was in shock and had to be sedated. We verified the papers and checked the room, but we found nothing. We waited for your arrival before going over the car."

"Inspector, we have reasons to believe that there's a fur coat containing stolen diamonds in the car. As far as Mrs. Popescu goes, we want to take her back to Romania. There's no charges against her."

"I will discuss it with my superiors. This is too much for now. Please, check the car. My colleagues will escort you. The Greek diamond expert, Frau Papastergiu, is on her way from the airport. She will be here in about forty-five minutes."

***

Pushkin checks his cigarettes. There's only a few left. He's been smoking too much but knows this job is getting close to the climax.

The last act will be played out in France. He mulls over thoughts of retirement. *In my job there's no such thing! Who knows, maybe I'm one of the last old school guys that could enjoy a few last years in peace. On a sunny island… Skiathos, or Mallorca…*

He pushes down a bit more on the gas as he drives down the highway. Paris is still far away. He debates stopping to grab something to eat. Maybe that long awaited schnitzel! He could buy a new pack of Dunhills and make a few phone calls.

As they go through the interior of the car, there's nothing of interest: cigarettes, gum, half-empty bottles of juice, a folded map, junk food and tissues. The trunk is next. Everyone crowds around as they pop it open. Inside are two medium-sized suitcases. An Austrian officer opens the first zipper. There's an envelope containing money. Lot of money, all in fifty euro bills. There's a few colourful brochures, two new shirts, an electric shaver, a map of South America, a cell phone with a charger, deodorant, tooth paste and a tooth brush.

"Packed for a quick escape, gentlemen. This lawyer didn't take chances. Here's our last chance."

The officer slowly unzips the second bag. Inside, there's a big, black plastic bag wrapped in brown packing tape. Someone offers a pocketknife and the plastic tears with a dull sound. Nobody breathes.

A fur coat cascades out of the package. It's decorated with six big, round and thick buttons. It's Tania Sevcenko's fur coat. *Finally!*

Jacques Sardi is bored. Turning over the many stages of his life, he's still not sure the source of his weariness. Maybe it's his job, his girl-friend or his old scratched desk. Or maybe it's the sludge they call coffee that comes from the vending machine. It's more likely that it's just too hot in Paris for the old air conditioner sputtering in his office.

His cases just aren't that interesting. Though he did get the chance to visit two seedy nightclubs and entertain himself with the Russian dancers and their attempts at speaking French. He asked if they came to Paris with fur coats from Romania. And he kept searching for this Jacques Colbert, the elusive character allegedly appearing and disappearing all over France and Eastern Europe.

Never heard a more stupid thing. Diamonds hidden in the buttons of fur coats, transported in a dancer's luggage. Of course the girls don't have furs and know nothing. All of this is a weak theory cooked up by my some Romanian cops looking to visit Paris on the government's tab...

A message appears on his laptop and brightens him up. A message from his commander.

If a Russian adviser named Mikhail Pushkin contacts you, please grant him your full support. He's involved in the diamonds investigation and represents the Russian government in Moscow. I'll send you all the details.

Please, control your emotions, I don't want problems with the Ministry.

Good luck.

Jacques Sardi smirks. His father left him to promote communism with a Soviet female doctor he had met during his Resistance years. It was 1956, and he was still a baby.

Too many cooks in the kitchen. Nothing good can come of this. He deletes the message. *Merde!*

As evening falls, the sky slowly shifts from purple to a dark blue. The French highways are busy. He's just passed Strasbourg, keeping a constant speed of 120 km/h. For the last fifteen minutes, he's certain he is being followed. A grey Renault Espace, steadily stays two vehicles behind. He changes lanes and speed, and the Renault follows suit. It could be paranoia from fatigue, but something tells him that the enemy will strike again.

If he missed me from a stationary position in Braşov, he'll try again on the go, or he'll wait for me to park somewhere isolated. He's desperate to stop me, but doesn't know how. He's out of practice.

Placing his gun on the passenger seat, he unfastens his seatbelt, slows down and waits for his tail's first move.

This time he'll have to play by my rules.

Eleni Papstergiu arrives in Pressbaum to find a fur coat stretched out on a table like a hunting trophy. Its buttons are exposed. Seven men form a circle around it, satisfaction painted all over their faces. None of them notice the new arrival until one of the policemen whispers something to the Austrian inspector. Steiner turns around.

Suddenly, the room stirs. The two Greeks exchange greetings and introductions are made, but silence quickly returns. Everybody waits for the expert's opinion.

Eleni smiles for the first time in hours.

"Gentlemen, you're wrong if you think I can find diamonds by looking at these buttons."

More silence.

"Well, let's remove them from the coat. At least a couple of them. I'll need a magnifying-glass and an X-ray, or an ultra-sound scanner. Wouldn't it have been easier to do this over at the police headquarters?"

"I apologize, Frau Papastergiu, but things happened so fast and overwhelmed us. I will prepare everything you've asked for, but it'll take some time," Inspector Steiner replies.

"You must at least have some a magnifying-glass. And I hope you don't expect me to break six plastic buttons."

"Unfortunately, we'll have to make do with whatever we can find on the spot."

Steiner barks a few orders in German. The rest of the group remains silent. A uniformed policeman detaches two buttons with a pocketknife and presents them to the Greek teacher along with a lamp and a powerful magnifier.

She observes them with an amused expression for a few moments, she pokes the tip of the knife into the tiny gap on the side of the button. The two plastic pieces snap open up and a small object rolls out from inside. Eleni picks it up.

"So This is why you brought me here?"

She holds a cherry pit between her thumb and forefinger.

The signs indicate that a rest area is coming up in 1,500 meters. He counts mentally: *1,000 metres... 500 metres...*

He slows down and opens the windows on the left side of the car. Easing to a crawl, he enters the rest area. There are no other cars, so no witnesses. He stops on the other side of the rest stop, close to the exit. He turns off the headlights and grabs his gun. The other car parks, killing the engine and lights. There are about fifty meters separating the two cars. It's dark, only the distant glow of passing cars fleetingly illuminates the rest stop.

The door of the Renault opens and shuts. Pushkin thinks he should get out too. The roar from the highway muffles the sound.

He slides over to the passenger side and gets out. He aims his gun in his right hand, and leaves his left for hand-to-hand. There's a suspicious *click* in the distance and he steps away from the Range Rover, trying to distinguish his opponent's shadow in the darkness. There's a sudden movement and a flash of light. It's too late to take cover. The explosion sends him crashing down as the Range Rover bursts into flames.

His attacker throws the RPG on the Renault's backseat and starts the engine. He drives past the fiery wreck and notices the body on the ground. He turns on his headlights and speeds up.

A few cars stop at the scene. Someone calls the police. Sirens close in.

FOURTEEN

IT'S EARLY MORNING AND THE AIR IS COOL. A LIGHT BREEZE slips in through the open windows of the sixth floor of a 19th century building. The view is spectacular—the Seine flows peacefully in the background, the Eiffel Tower sits in the distance and Sacré-Cœur Basilica watches over the city on top of the hill of Montmartre.

Stelian arrives at a police briefing room and sips the all too familiar bitter coffee.

He has to pull himself out of his reverie. He hadn't dreamed he'd end up in Paris. People were in silence, typing on laptops, writing reports over coffee. A wave of nausea overcomes Munteanu. He finds it hard to eat in the morning. *Though an omelet would have been nice*, he laughs inwardly. Despite his stomach, he grabs a fresh croissant and pours himself a black coffee.

It's been one day since they left Austria. One long day. After being told that Pushkin was attacked outside of Strasbourg, Theodopoulos, Eleni Papastergiu and himself left Vienna for Paris. Toni Demetriade escorted Nora Popescu back to Romania. French policeman Jacques Sardi is doing his best to manage the crisis. Such a brutal attack is very unusual in France. Despite all of this, Jacques Colbert and Mircea Popescu are nowhere to be found. And nobody knows where the diamonds are or when they replaced the buttons on the fur coat.

"Gentlemen, may I please have your attention."

Sardi watches his three foreign guest stood next to some plain-clothes French detectives.

"I will try to sum up everything we know for certain and where we're at right now. Jacques Colbert and Mircea Popescu are still on the loose. They're armed and have money. Eight days ago Colbert sold some of his shares for a total value of 120000 euro. No doubt they have more funds after selling at least ten diamonds last year. They are, most likely, in the possession of another six diamonds."

"We suspect that they have multiple vehicles rented under different identities. The two cars belonging to Colbert are now parked in the underground garage of his Paris residence. A Renault Espace, containing a Romanian manufactured AG 7 RPG, was found abandoned less than fifty kilometres away from the scene of the attack on Pushkin. If it was the work of Colbert, he had transportation waiting to get away. The Renault was registered in Strasbourg and was stolen a few hours earlier. We found no finger-prints. We placed surveillance teams at Colbert's other properties, even at addresses where we know he lived for short periods of time. Unfortunately, he's a loner who travels extensively."

He pauses to sip from his cup of coffee.

"The only solid clue we have is a building he owns in Rouen, close to the train station. It's an old five-story building. Colbert started to renovate it and brought in Romanian construction workers. We have reasons to believe that he has a hiding place in this building. Right now there are eight people working there, supervised by a French foreman. We haven't approached them, since we don't want them to know we're watching the building. We have five surveillance points working around the clock. That's all, thank you."

"What exactly do you intend to do?" Munteanu asks.

"Although time is short, for now, we wait."

"The eight workers are registered with the police?"

"Yes, monsieur Munteanu."

"And you have their pictures?"

"Yes. They received work permits from the Internal Affairs Ministry."

"Can we see them?"

"Certainly. I will take care of it."

"One more thing. What do you know about the French manager coordinating the renovation?"

"We have his name and information. He's employed by a French construction company. A very important and respectable company."

"Any pictures?"

"No, but we can find one. What do you need it for?"

"I have a gut feeling. One of the workers could be Popescu, and the French foreman could be Colbert. It's an easy for them to hide in the building unnoticed. Plus, they could supervise building more hiding places, maybe even some tunnels for an emergency escape."

Sardi starts to laugh loudly.

"Monsieur Munteanu, I think you've read too many crime books! Let's not exaggerate! These delinquents can't think that far ahead."

"Well they seem smart enough to have eluded you until now!"

Theodopulous steps in:

"Gentlemen, this is hardly the time or place to argue. We need to be proactive. Inspector, please ask for all pictures and check to see if all of the workers showed up for work today."

The traffic of people around the market of the Rouen train station slowly build. Office workers carrying big bags scuttle off to their jobs, while tourists juggle their luggage and cameras as they descend the arriving trains. It's an obstacle course to avoid flower stands, newspaper kiosks and coffee shop tables on the sidewalks.

The grey building undergoing a thorough renovation nearby is surrounded by scaffolding. Part of the tile roof is missing and replaced by plastic covers. The last two floors have no windows. The construction site is fenced in wood hoarding. At the entrance, there are a few oversized tanks with *Inflammable* warnings written on the sides. On the old, crooked door, there's a huge metal lock below a handwritten notice.

A man dressed in dark blue workman's overalls, a cap and an old briefcase i stops in front of the entrance and unlocks the door. He goes inside, but comes back a few moments later, pushing a cart to pick up one of the metal cans. Ten minutes later he comes out again, loads up another can and goes back inside.

Two men watch him carefully from a Gas de France truck parked behind a flower stand. One of them takes pictures with an 800 mm telephoto lens, trying to get a clear shot of the man's face. They email the pictures to as soon as they're taken.

Back in Paralia, the murder has faded from memory for most people. Only Theodopoulos' colleagues are reminded thanks to their longer work hours. In Bucharest, Toni Demetriade tries unsuccessfully to obtain a statement from Nora Popescu. Still in shock, she was transported straight from the airport to a hospital emergency. Her lawyers then stepped in. Daniel Manole, her brother, is the only one allowed to see her, but he fails to get her to talk. The doctors decide to keep her under observation, worrying that the shock could provoke a suicide attempt.

The Romanian media have set their sights on the story, debating the finer points of the case. Two TV channels try to invite Daniel on to one talk-show after another, but, on advice from his lawyer, he declines giving any statements or interviews.

The Romanian police also decide to invoke the so-called *silenzio stampa*, making all material pertaining to the case strictly confidential due to their ongoing investigation. At the Montmartre, life goes on. After giving three interviews, Galia is bombarded with film offers and marriage proposals. She hasn't made it to Paris... *It's never too late!*

Sitting in the back seats of a car, Stelian and Eleni chat quietly. They've discovered common passions: coin collecting and photography. In the front seats, Sardi and Theodopoulos review surveillance pictures one more time. There has only been one worker on the construction site, the same one that had carried around the cannisters. The French foreman hasn't shown up at all. But the pictures say little. The worker's face was mostly hidden by his hat and beard. While on site, he mainly carried the cannisters around for a while, then left.

"I'm afraid the only solution is to get into that site and take a look around."

"Monsieur Sardi, I doubt you can get a search warrant at this hour," Theodopoulos counters.

"So we'll pay a visit off the record."

"OK. I'll come with you."

"But of course."

It's almost midnight and pretty quiet in the market. There's only coffee house patrons and couples in love. Their car is parked on a little side street, about a hundred metres from the entrance to the house. Sardi grabs his binoculars and carefully scans every window and then back to the entrance door one more time.

"Looks quiet and locked up. I want to know what's written on that piece of paper attached to the door."

"Well, let's go and see then. You two coming?"

Stelian and Eleni don't answer, they're lost in discussion about photography and night exposure.

"We've lost them. It's just you and me, monsieur Sardi."

The Frenchman checks his gun.

"Are you armed, Mr. Theodopoulos?"

"Yes."

He shows Sardi the Smith & Wesson at his waist.

"Let's go then."

They open the car doors simultaneously. Stelian jumps.

"Where are you two going?"

"To check out something. If we're not back in ten minutes, dial 110 on the communication panel for help."

"Okay. Good luck."

The two men walk away. Stelian and Eleni remain quiet. Munteanu touches the Beretta at his waist. The last time he'd touched it, he was also next to a beautiful woman. Eleni smiles at him in the darkness and he reaches out to caress her hair.

That same moment they hear a loud shot ring out from the house and lights switch on from the first and second floors. Out on the street, nobody seems to have noticed.

FIFTEEN

THE MAN JUMPS. HE'S VERY SENSITIVE LATELY. HIS NERVES ARE frayed. He's waiting in a Renault Twingo, parked behind a small truck in the train station market. His heart starts to beat faster at the familiar noise and he watches as the lights are turned on in the house.

On the passenger seat there's small arsenal of weapons. He slips the thin knife in a special sheath attached to his left boot, then places his two guns—a small Smith & Wesson pistol and his 10 mm Glock—in holsters under his arm and at his waist. He's dressed in black. Only the fluorescent Sector watch is visible in the darkness. He covers it with his sleeve and silently opens his door. But he doesn't leave the car.

"Something happened!" Eleni exclaims.

"I think so."

"Let's call for help!"

"It could be too late. I'll go in."

Stelian takes out his weapon.

"I'll go with you."

"It's too dangerous."

Eleni smiles and gives him a quick kiss.

"I'm coming."

The kiss takes him by surprise. He hesitates for a moment. Then smiles.

"Okay. Let's go!"

They both get out of the car and run to the entrance. The door is open. On the paper it's written: *Renovation suspended for 48 hours. Waiting for Supplies.*

"So that's why the workers didn't come today."

"One of them did though!"

"Maybe he's the one getting the supplies."

They open the door, which squeaks on its hinges. Inside is a dusty hallway, filled with debris and trash. A few workers' uniforms hang from an improvised hanger. There are stairs and an elevator is stopped at the ground floor with no door. Coloured wires pour out of the light switches, everything is illuminated by a weak light bulb hanging from the ceiling. Two doors on either side lead to ground floor apartments. Munteanu tries the door handles but they're locked.

"Let's go to the first floor," he whispers.

The old stairs squeak. They find one of the doors open when they reach the first floor. Light comes from inside. As they creep closer to get a better look the barrel of a gun emerges out of the darkness and is shoved sharply in Munteanu's side. It's followed by a familiar voice whispering in Romanian:

"Nice to meet you again, Mr. Journalist. Put that toy on the floor and get in here."

Eleni tries to run, but the man blocks her way.

"Same goes for you lady."

They step over the threshold, pushed from behind by the armed man. The room is spacious and barely furnished. There's only a wooden table and four chairs. In a corner, two metal cans. Jacques Sardi and Theodopoulos are tied up on two of the chairs, thick tape covering their mouths. The Greek's right sleeve is drenched in blood; it trickles down his hand and onto the dusty floor.

"Don't worry about him. He's not wounded badly and besides, it doesn't matter anymore."

A cold shiver runs down Munteanu's spine. What does he mean it doesn't it matter anymore? His life flashes by in a second, stopping at the kiss from a few minutes before. It seems like a dream.

"I pegged you as the post-revolutionary opportunist type of crook, Mr. Popescu, not a common thug."

"You use heavy words, Mr. Munteanu, but as I said, it doesn't matter anymore."

Popescu handcuffs them, then ties their legs.

"No tape for our mouths?"

"Maybe I want to chat a bit, Mr. Journalist. There's still a few things I want to clear up."

"I can't help you there. Nothing's clear to me."

"Sarcasm is outdated, Mr. Journalist. I only want my diamonds."

Popescu removes the tape from Theodopoulos and Sardi's mouths. He continues, this time in French:

"I want to know what have you done with my diamonds?!"

The four hostages exchange surprised looks.

"Here's my problem. The diamonds were hidden in Tania's fur coat. I didn't have time to confirm it that night, or on my way to Romania. Only when I arrived to Bucharest did I find out the diamonds had been replaced with cherry seeds. This means the French Police are out of the equation. That leaves the Greek and Romanian Police. I'm listening, gentlemen!"

"That's really stupid. How could we have switched the diamonds if we never touched the coat? Where did you keep the coat that night?"

"After my discussion with Tania, I—"

"You mean after you poisoned her!"

"She knew too much and was blackmailing me. She wanted out and was charming my brother-in-law. I don't like violence, but she didn't leave me much choice. I took the fur coat and placed it in the trunk of my car. In the morning I packed it in my suitcase."

"Then none of us could have done anything. We had no idea that a murder had taken place."

"Murder?! What an ugly word! I prefer self-preservation. Tania knew what she was getting herself into from the beginning. She accepted everything. The coat stayed in the suitcase at the Themis Hotel for a day. That's when the switch must have taken place. The room was empty for quite some time. We left the next night."

"But the investigation had barely started and we knew nothing about diamonds. There was no motive, we had nothing. Daniel Manole was under arrest," Iannis Theodopoulos remarks as he discretely pulls his legs under the chair.

Eleni watches him from the corner of her eye. Next to her chair there's a pole from a shovel leaning on an old heater. She stays out of the discussion and tries to lean her chair backwards trying to reach for it. The Greek policeman gently rocks his chair. If he could slam into the table in front of him, he could knock Popescu down. Munteanu knows he has to distract Popescu. Sardi flexes his muscles and Munteanu notices how he removes a short piece of metal from his watch wristband and slips it into the handcuffs' lock. The light is dim enough and Popescu is too tired to realize what's going on. Stelian smiles.

"What's so funny, Mr. Munteanu? In ten minutes I will set off a bomb. The explosion won't be big, but it'll be enough to ignite the cans of varnish. There are two more cans in the room above us. The fire will be unstoppable. By the time the firefighters arrive, you'll be charred to a crisp."

Another cold shiver crosses Munteanu. The thought that he might actually die terrifies him. And didn't even get to enjoy his last vacation. Eleni is now inches away from the shovel pole. All four of them are on edge.

Popescu forces a laugh.

"Even if you try something stupid, a bullet will do just as well as a fire. Don't think I wouldn't do it. That is unless you give me the diamonds."

"You must be really stupid if you don't understand that we don't have them," Munteanu replies, irritated. "The only man who knew everything and always acted alone was Misha Pushkin, but either you or Colbert took care of him with an RPG."

Sardi interferes:

"But, Colbert doesn't even exist, right?"

Popescu grins.

"You figured that one out too huh?"

"It wasn't too hard. Colbert is always in France; Popescu is always in Romania, and nobody ever saw Colbert. A convenient double identity."

"It doesn't matter anymore. In a few hours I'll be far away. My only regret is not having the six diamonds. My collection would have been complete."

Eleni touches the rod just as Sardi succeeds in opening the lock of his cuffs. Iannis Theodopoulos keeps rocking. Popescu grins again and steps back exactly when the Greek man's chair slams into the table. Eleni grabs the rod and Sardi jumps forward, but it's too late. Popescu is already out of the room and is locking the door behind him.

There's a sharp whizz and a red light blinks on a black box that looks like a pack of cigarettes on a metal cans.

"Quickly, throw it out!" yells Sardi.

SIXTEEN

JUST AT THAT MOMENT, THE LIGHTS GO OUT. THEY CAN HEAR noises coming from the stairs, yelling and then a barrage of gun shots. Someone unlocks the door and the beam a flashlight on the four hostages.

"Everyone OK? We've got to hurry. The bomb will go off in seven or eight minutes. I have the keys to the handcuffs."

The man in black pulls out a bunch of keys from his pocket and silently sets everyone free. Sardi had already unlocked his.

"The French police trained you very well, inspector."

Sardi mumbles something. Everyone hurries toward the exit.

"What about Popescu? What happened?"

"He's dead."

They can hear the sirens. The place is surrounded and roped off by police, a bomb squad, multiple ambulances and firefighters. But they're too late. The bomb detonates and the fire spreads. Firefighters step in promptly with water and foam hoses. Munteanu and his companions are seated on the grass in a small park right across the street from the train station.

The man in black takes out a pack of Dunhills and a golden lighter from his pocket, lights a cigarette and smokes silently.

"I really should quit."

"Don't you think you owe us an explanations Mr. Pushkin?"

Pushkin laughs. No one ever sees him laugh out loud.

"Yes, you have the right to know. It's actually very simple. It all started thirty years ago. Mircea Popescu was a colleague of mine. I was even his mentor for a little while. We were in the KGB back then. After the earthquake in March 1977 we sent him in to Romania. We were on bad terms with your country then, and Ceausescu hunted us relentlessly. We created a state-of-the-art cover story for Popescu...school, family, everything. From then on it was easy. Or so we thought. He started secretly working for the other side. We'll never know how much he played us both and your Securitate. After 1989, he went freelance. Foreign businesses, Colbert, the import-export company, the yacht, then the diamonds. He was a genius, but never knew when and where to stop. It's how it always happens with guys like that. If he would have stopped after the first six diamonds, he would have gotten away with it. But he wanted more. And he fell in love with that girl, Tania Sevcenko. Such a hardened man, but Tatiana played him perfectly. Then she started to blackmail him and set him off by getting involved with Daniel Manole. Maybe she really loved him. I don't know. I think he killed her out of jealousy. The lawyer was just a fool in the whole thing, he wanted Nora..."

He remains silent for a few moments and removes a flat bottle from his pocket.

"Metaxa cognac, five stars. I bought it the night he killed her. I was too late to stop him. That's when I knew what he'd become and how dirty he could play. It's my fault. Then we went back and forth, both of us waiting for the other to make the smallest mistake. Like chess."

He takes a good swig from the bottle, then offers it to the others.

"It's all over now. Nora will recover. She's young and now she's rich. I don't even think she loved him that much. Maybe at the beginning. Popescu and I, we were the last old school guys left out there. Now it's just me. I think it's time I step out as well. I bid you farewell."

"What about all the set up with your death? The RPG?"

"Actually, it wasn't a set up. It was very, very close. I don't even know if he wanted to kill me, or just warn me. I took advantage of the situation, but I don't think he bought it. Or maybe he did ... I'll never know. I'm getting old."

He removes the gun from his underarm holster and throws it on the grass.

"I had to shoot him twice to get him. So long."

Pushkin gets to his feet, lights a new cigarette and walks away. Munteanu jumps to his feet and follows him.

"Wait! What about the diamonds?"

Pushkin looks him straight in the eye.

"What diamonds?"

Puskin gets into his car, starts the engine and takes off. Stelian looks pensively after the car. He passes a hand through his hair and mutters:

"Yeah, as he said, if Popescu stopped at the first six diamonds, he would have gotten away with it. Now, this second set of diamonds will fund Pushkin's retirement quite nicely."

SEVENTEEN

IT'S EARLY OCTOBER AND THE END OF HIGH SEASON FOR tourists. The sun is weaker now and the Piralia harbour is not filled with people anymore. No more improvised camping from tourists sleeping outside on the docks. The huge ferryboats are docked in tidy lines, like gigantic hippos waiting to dry.

Eleni is seated on a bench. Young, beautiful and now in love. She's surrounded by luggage. They're only leaving for two weeks, but they're carrying half the house with them. Her house. Two weeks alone on a deserted islands. No bosses, no friends…

Discover the Greek Islands…that's what was written on those colour-ful posters at the police station. They clearly left a mark! I can't believe a year has already gone by. The return home. My resignation. The mes-sages going back and forth between me and Eleni. No word from the others. Only a Skiathos postal card from Pushkin at the beginning of April…just a few words: I'm waiting for you! Stupid! Now I've left everything behind. No more playing the policeman! I'm an editor now.

Stelian looks for a restroom. *I had a bit too much beer last night, dreaming of this trip.* He stops in front of a restaurant. A Greek man, probably working as both a bodyguard and a bartender, offers him a polite, but inquiring smile. Munteanu sighs nervously.

"Do you speak English? Parlez-vous français? Parlare italiano?"

The Greek man shrugs, amused at each question. Munteanu feels helpless. The situation is a little tense. He finally explodes:

"The hell with it! It's so damn difficult to find a restroom around here!"

The Greek guy's smile widens.

"Why didn't you say that from the beginning? I speak Romanian, I was born in Brăila. The restroom is in the back, left side."

"Thank you!"

Munteanu hurries in the direction indicated. In forty min-utes they will board the ferryboat. And by tonight, they'll already be in their room. An elegant room with a sea-view terrace in a big, white villa. A romantic dinner on the beach, the breeze caressing them, Eminescu, candles and fresh flowers, sirtaki in the background, uzo, caviar, Greek salad, tzatziki, Metaxa and then…*Maybe a night of making love, just the two of us and the moonlight…*

He remembers other lovers. *Not a happy ending for them!* He steps back, at the last moment avoiding the restroom door as another man exits.

His phone rings. He freezes in front of the door. *Oh, God, not again!* He takes out his cell phone, watching it worriedly. Not a number from Romania. Someone calling him from somewhere else. He turns around, terrified, and takes a few steps toward the exit. He tries to concentrate. *What should I do? Do I answer or not?* The Greek guy from Brăila greets him amiably, but he barely notices. He tries to locate the number. *France, Germany, Italy?*

He finally answers. He's outside now. A few feet away, Eleni, tanned and dressed in a colourful, revealing dress, smiles at him invitingly.

"Hello?"

"Bonjour, mon cher. Jacques Sardi t'appelle."

For a moment, he's happy to hear the voice of the French inspector, but after another moment he freezes. There's no reason in the world why Sardi would call him. *Damn it, this is serious!*

"What's up, Jacques?"

"Are you in a hurry?"

"Actually, yes. I'm in Piralia with Eleni. We're leaving for a vacation in half an hour. You didn't call me without a reason. What happened?"

"I see. So you two decided to spend some time alone. Congratulations, mon ami! Should we expect a wedding some time soon?"

"Cut the crap, Sardi. What the hell has happened?"

"OK OK, I won't beat around the bush."

He pauses, as if he's trying to find the courage to speak.

"We have a problem."

"I knew it. And?"

"I'm in Germany right now. Frankfurt. Frankfurt Main, to be exact. There's an international book fair opening here tomorrow. I told you I was planning to go, remember?"

"Yes, I do. And?"

"You probably won't forgive me for the rest of your life if I continue."

"Stop bullshitting me, Sardi! Tell me!"

"Okay, I'll give you a brief. Two hours ago a body was found in the French bookstand, hidden behind a curtain. The man was hired by a German company to work in the building."

"And what does all this have to do with me?"

"Well...the guy was Romanian."

"Uggggh."

"My bosses asked me to call you. The German Police agreed."

"What about the Romanian Police?"

"For now the chief inspector doesn't know anything. You've resigned. And you're on vacation now."

"Thanks for screwing up another vacation."

"Look, we only need you for a couple days. We'll solve everything quickly."

"But the press will talk about it."

"No, they won't. It's all under wraps. There's nothing political to worry about. Especially now...with all the European Union crap..."

"But I don't have any—"

"Please, help us, Stelian. This is a very delicate matter. Help me and then ask for anything you want!"

"Fine, whatever. But like I said, I'm in the harbour with Eleni. We were supposed to sail for the islands."

"Where exactly are you, Athens or Salonica?"

"Piralia."

"Take a taxi to the airport. I'll take care of everything. Two flight tickets on your names will be waiting for you at the Lufthansa stand. Please, hurry! I'll owe you for life for this one! Bon voyage!"

The connection ends but Munteanu still holds the phone next to his ear. He takes a few steps. Eleni stands and approaches him.

"Who was on the phone? What happened?"

"You won't believe this. Call a taxi, please. We're going to the airport."

"What?! The airport? What about our vacation on the islands?"

"We'll go. Someday…"

He takes her hand and pulls her into his arms. He lightly kisses her lips…fills himself with her aroma.

"Let me go! Tell me! You won't get away with it that easily!"

"Okay. It was Jacques Sardi. Please, Eleni, call for a taxi. Our flight tickets are waiting for us at the airport."

"But why?"

"Right, I still haven't told you. There was a murder in Frankfurt…a Romanian guy. They need me."

"Good Lord! Will we ever get some peace?"

Stelian sighs and shrugs.

"I don't know, my darling. I'm starting to wonder if it's a curse?"

They gather their luggage and walk toward the exit of the harbour. The sun is gaining strength as it beats down on them…

Acknowledgements

My thanks to all my Romanian friends, authors and readers, especially to Lucia Verona and Monica Ramirez, a great translator. I would also like to thank Ramona Mitrică, Mike Phillips and Mihai Râșnovean from ProFusion, my first English-language publishers. My gratitude to Quentin Bates, Barry Forshaw, Jeffrey Siger and Sarah Ward and of course for my Canadian publishers from Mosaic Press, Howard Aster, Matthew Goody and Eric Normann.